Calamity Jane - How the West Began

Calamity Jane

How the West Began

Bryan Ney

Published 2017 by Creativia
Cover art by Andrew Brown // DesignForWriters.com

Dedicated to Nathaniel Pitt Langford, Montana Pioneer, Businessman, Worshipful Master Mason, Vigilante, Conservationist, Public Servant and Historian

Acknowledgements—and the Evolution of this Story

I am indebted to the generous advice and support of many people in the writing of this story. More than twenty years ago, through my wife Lisa, I met our friend and writer David Titcher, who was always encouraging, and tilted my emphasis from the underlying history to the importance of story in historical fiction. Midway through the project came Vartkes Cholakian, a filmmaker of boundless enthusiasm, whose unwavering belief in my writing provided moral support that kept me moving forward. Two to three years ago I decided to change the protagonist of the story from the doctor to Calamity Jane, and switch from a screenplay to a novel. David thought that would at least help me focus on character, and it did. The story flowed much easier than prior iterations. Research for this new direction led me to Ursula Smith, who had co-written *The Gold Rush Widows of Little Falls.* Ursula put me in touch with touch with Charlotte Orr, granddaughter of the Andrew Fergus of my story. Charlotte filled in some historical details and enthusiastically volunteered to be my unofficial publicist. Soon (in the context of a twenty-plus year project) I had a manuscript that needed input from others. Here I would like to thank my daughter Rayna for her early input ("Dad, she's too whiny," etc.). Story has to take primacy in historical fiction, but if too many liberties are taken, the story will grate on those who know the history best. I am very appreciative of the input of Ellen Baumler of the Montana Historical Society for her input in this regard. Around the same time I contacted Richard Etulain, foremost expert and author of several books on Calamity Jane. Richard generously agreed to read my manuscript and gave valuable feedback. Now I needed an editor, and was fortunate through the indispensable modern convenience of an internet search to find my editor and publisher, Jon VanZile of Dragon Tree Books. Jon's suggestions were right at the level needed by a first-time author and greatly enhanced the story. Useful advice on the craft of writing came from my neighbor, Leslie Lehr, a Novel Consultant whom I met by chance when trimming trees between our properties. Next came Andrew Brown of Writers by Design who created a "killer" cover and my website http://www.bryanney.com/. Lastly, with a nearly finished product in hand, comes my beta readers. Among several of those, I would like to especially thank Toni Edwards and Andrew Shaner for their incisive input and enthusiastic support.

I started with mention of my wife Lisa, and would like to end thanking her, as without her support and encouragement all these many years, this project would not have been the joy it has been.

Prologue

To support herself in her later years, Calamity Jane sold her ghost-written biography to passersby. Modern historians view that thin pamphlet as an interesting mixture of fact and fiction. In that bio, Calamity largely neglects her youth in the Montana goldfields, leaving a gap in her narrative. This story is how she might have filled that gap, had she thought you would believe her.

July, Civil War Era

The scant light of dusk ebbed from Bannack, civilization's most tenuous toehold in the Rocky Mountain wilderness. Rude log structures clustered on one side of a creek, capped by dirt and sod roofs, on one of which a pair of crows hopped and cawed at one another. Inside, Jane Canary, a sturdy-looking girl of fifteen, bent over a steaming pot on a sheet-iron stove, wooden spoon in hand. Jane was proud that she had been able to stretch to day's end the meager rations her parents had left.

"I'm hungry," said sister Lana.

Jane glanced at Lana, her face all innocence and light. A sprinkle of dirt was shaken loose from the ceiling. "Damn crows," muttered Jane. She glanced at the pole ceiling, then where the dirt had fallen near Queenie, their big yellow dog. Queenie nudged her recently weaned puppies and gave Jane a big sigh.

"I'm hungry, too, Lana," said Jane. "Don't worry, we'll eat in a minute, and then it's your bedtime."

"Is Ma gonna be okay?" Lana asked.

"She'll be fine," said Jane. But she could only mouth those words; there was no certainty behind them. Typhoid fever had laid Charlotte Canary awfully low in the past few days. Ma had finally decided to go to the doctor that morning before she might be too weak to make the short trip over the hill. Jane stirred the pot absent-mindedly, listening to the wind as it whistled through cracks in the walls. She bunched up the hem of her slip and used that to pick up the pot, then headed to the door to inspect it. A gunshot cracked through the dusk, and the crows took flight. Unfortunately for the girls, one of the birds was directly above where Jane held the pot, for a big clump of dirt plopped into the pot of beans.

"Goddamn it!" said Jane, as her body tensed, and her jaw clenched.

"Pa says you shouldn't swear," said Lana.

"Like he should talk," said Jane, casting her glance to a half-empty whiskey bottle in one corner of the squalid disarray of their cabin. She gingerly tried to fish the dirt out of the pot with the spoon, but the blunt end of this clumsy instrument only crushed the clump. She dropped the spoon and reached into the pot with fingers, trying to salvage their meal.

"Shit! Goddamn it!" she said, her hand jerking away reflexively, followed by a burning sensation lancing up her arm.

"Jane is a potty mouth, Jane is a potty mouth," Lana teased.

"Yeah, what of it?" Jane snapped as she set the pot back on the stove and blew on her injured hand.

Lana went wide-eyed, and her lower lip started to tremble. "I'm sorry."

"Ah, Lana, don't be sorry," said Jane, trying to avert the cascade of tears that was sure to follow.

"I'm trying to be good," Lana cried.

"You're being so good," said Jane. She swept to her sobbing sister's side and hugged her. Jane took the hem of her sister's flimsy cotton slip and dabbed tears away.

"I want my Ma," wailed Lana.

"Shush, shush there," said Jane, casting an eye out the door. A canvas flap was all that separated inside from out. "The neighbors will hear you."

"I don't care. They hate us. All the neighbors hate us."

"Here, Lana, I'll feed you, then you'll feel better."

Lana wiped away her tears and sat on the buffalo hide that covered part of the dirt floor, ready soon to be wrapped around the two of them as their bed. Jane took her knife out and in what light there was at the door she dug around in the bean pot, dabbing as many beans as she could onto a tin plate. "Here," she said.

Lana took the plate and scooped up the beans with her fingers, placing them in her mouth, licking her fingers on the way out. After a couple of chews, Lana screwed her face up and spit the beans out on the floor.

"Lana, don't do that," said Jane. "We got enough mice in here already."

"I don't care, you try it. It's all dirt."

Jane teased a few more beans out of the pot and placed them in her mouth. The beans crunched in her back teeth, and she spit them out on the ground outside. She grabbed the pot from the stove again and took it to the doorway. It was hopeless. "Okay, Lana. I guess it's just bedtime then."

"I can't go to bed," said Lana. "I'm still hungry. Where's Pa?"

"Across the creek. He'll be back in the morning," Jane said. Visons of gold had lured Pa to Bannack from distant Missouri, but the good claims were all gone by the time they had arrived. A farmer by rade, now he turned to gambling.

"I'm hungry now," said Lana. "We gotta find Pa."

"I can't leave you here and just go across the creek and get him," said Jane. The late arrivals to the goldfields like the Canary family mostly lived on this side of the creek, the saloons and the early arrivals were on the other.

"Good. I'll go with you," said Lana.

There was a muffled gunshot, and simultaneously a dull "plunk" in their wall towards town. A little chinked mud cascaded to the floor to confirm the hit.

"It's not safe, Lana," said Jane.

"You're a chicken. I'll go by myself."

"Lana, you are only six."

"Next year I'll be seven, and you'll prob'ly still be a chicken."

Lana knew how to goad her older sister, who prided herself in being fearless.

"All right. Then get your dollie," said Jane.

"Really?"

"Yeah, really. I'll teach you who's chicken." Queenie nuzzled Jane as Lana scurried for her doll. She was a good hunting dog, with coarse fur not meant to be petted. "You stay, old girl, and be a good Ma to them puppies," Jane said, scratching behind Queenie's ears. She went to the doorway to examine her hand, where blisters confirmed what the throbbing told her. A neighbor woman returned home with a bucket of water. The woman, one who had travelled the months-long journey from St. Louis with the Canary's, was lit by an interior candle for a moment when she opened her door. She gave Jane a stern look, then hurried inside. Lana took Jane's good hand, clutching her corncob doll to her chest with her other hand. The girls passed through the canvas flaps and started their journey. Jane shivered as the breeze passed through the thin slip that was all that stood between her and the elements.

Violin music struggled to make itself known above the din coming from the saloons. The violins that the girls heard would have been musical if each instrument had been enjoyed in isolation, but the sound of several at the same time sounded like competing cats in heat. Combined with shouting and singing, occasionally punctuated by gunshots, this noise now served as the beacon that guided Jane and Lana to an uncertain destination. Scant steps from home, the girls came to the Salt Lake City Road, which they followed towards the creek. Water gurgled through long wooden troughs, sluices which the miners used to separate creek-bed gravel from the denser gold they coveted. The creek was shallow enough to be easily forded by horses and wagons, but for foot traffic there were two logs, hewn flat on top and worn smooth already over the few months of Bannack's existence.

Jane took a step up on the bridge and offered her hand to Lana. "Come on," she said.

"I'm scared," Lana said, twisting away with her doll clutched close. The crack of another gunshot pierced the night air.

Jane tried to stop shivering so her voice would sound more reassuring. "Lana, we gotta find Pa," she coaxed, her hand outstretched. "I won't let you fall."

Lana took Jane's hand, and the sisters shuffled sideways across the bridge to the midpoint. The doll that Lana held so tightly was months old now, so it was beginning to fall apart. It was due to being held so

tightly that now, ironically, its foot fell off and into a fold of Lana's dress. "Oh, no," cried Lana. "My dollie!"

She bent down to pick up the foot, but in so doing the small fold flattened out and the doll's foot plunked into the stream. "My dollie's foot!" Lana cried as the stream swiftly carried it away.

"It's gone, Lana," said Jane. "Let's go."

"My dollie needs her foot," said Lana, and she stamped her feet and pouted.

"I'll look for it in the morning," said Jane. "Right now we gotta go."

"Look for it now," Lana demanded, and stamped her feet again. Lana's feet slipped on the wet log and she lost her balance, bending at the waist, flailing her arms in the air. Jane quickly grabbed her sister by the waist, flung her over her shoulder and took two steps on the log before she lost her own balance. She made a leap for the far stream bank, but landed short, splashing on her bottom at the creek edge, pulling Lana into her lap at the same time.

"Lana," said Jane, "now look at us. You know you have to mind me when Ma and Pa aren't home."

"I told you, I'm trying to be good."

"Well, fine," said Jane. "Let's go find Pa."

They brushed off mud the best they could, and Jane wrung water out of her skirt. The sisters continued up Main Street, keeping to the edge to avoid the center that reeked of draft animal manure and urine. They passed a cluster of homes belonging to the early arrivals to the area, protected from errant bullets in a little hollow. These homes had a more substantial appearance than the rude and hastily built homes of

Jane's neighborhood. Some even had small windows of greased paper to let in light. Envy distracted Jane for just a moment, but she quickly pressed on.

The wilds around town were Jane's natural element and where she spent most of her time, but she had been on Main Street once or twice before. She compared her recollection of those forays to what now lay before her in the dark. The brewery, the bakery, and the dry goods store were closed and it was hard to tell which was which, but no matter, that. It was from the multiple saloons interspersed among these businesses that Jane had to choose.

The dust of the street turned to grime on the girls' wet feet, extending halfway to their knees. Lana started to whimper again. "Maybe we should go find Ma instead."

"Ma is too sick. We got to find Pa." Jane shivered uncontrollably for a moment, as her wet slip clung to her skin. "We're almost there," she said, as if she knew. But how was she to guess where Pa was? It was no help that signs graced the fronts of some of the saloons, just so much wasted lumber and paint to an illiterate farm girl. Jane peered in the door of the nearest saloon. Of all of them, this one had the most civilized façade, with two rows of pane glass windows on both sides of the door. No music came from within this one, only a steady stream of shouted threats and curses, as if every man within it wanted to prove he was the baddest man in a bad town. Jane decided to try the next one instead. Cursing and shouting flowed from that one as well, but at least the epithets she heard had a sense of humor and celebration to them. This place was crowded to overflowing, though, so Jane led Lana onward.

Jane scanned her remaining choices and was drawn to the one across the street. This place had a much less agitated appearance than the others, and the loudest sound coming from it was the violin music. So Jane and Lana carefully picked their way across the rutted street to this establishment, mud and manure squeezing between their toes. Jane stopped just short of the doorway and looked at Lana in the dim light that came from within. She grimaced at her sister's grimy face and tattered, muddy slip, knowing that her own appearance must be just as disheveled. Already scorned on her side of the creek, she did not want more of the same on this side now. Nor worse, pity.

"Lana, here," she said. She pulled her sister close, and with the cleanest part of her dress she could find, tried to wipe days of grime and neglect from Lana's face.

"Are we there yet?" asked Lana.

"Yeah, this is prob'ly it," Jane said. She grasped her sister's hand, took a breath, and pushed open the door to the saloon with a determined thrust.

Screeching violin music washed over them as they stepped inside. Jane's blinking eyes searched quickly. The smell of cigars and something foreign and spicy was so intense that it made her nose sting and her eyes water. The violin player saw the girls first and stopped midnote, bow pointed to the ceiling like an exclamation point. Bearded men in remnants of clothing from former lives turned from their card games one by one and stared in silence. Jane felt exposed in her scant clothing, and embarrassed that they were both so dirty, despite her efforts.

A Chinese woman with a modicum of faded beauty rose from dealing cards, revealing her shiny silk dress with ornate embroidery. "I am Madam Chi," spoke the exotic woman. "How may I help?"

"I am looking for my Pa, ma'am," said Jane.

Madam Chi nodded. "His name?"

"Bob Canary, ma'am."

A Chinese man with a long pigtail came to Madam Chi's side. She continued. "And your name?"

"Jane Canary, ma'am."

"Is there here a Bob Canary?" Madam Chi asked the room.

A greasy-looking character in a tattered gray military uniform growled, "He don't frequent this joint."

Jane had half expected this, and was ready to turn tail and try the next saloon, but Lana was not prepared for such disappointment. Her lower lip started to tremble.

"I want my Pa!" she cried.

Jane saw pity in the eyes of the men, and the greasy man in the military garb gave her a look that made her feel vulnerable. "Come on, Lana, he must be next door." Before the tears could cascade, she picked up her sister by her waist and rushed out the door.

The violin player resumed his merry tune. "Now there's a calamity if I ever saw one," he said.

Madam Chi conferred with her pigtailed partner, who nodded and left by the back door.

Outside, Jane ran across the rutted street. She stumbled and fell to her knees in the filth, dropping Lana.

"Yuck. Where are we going?" whined Lana.

"Next door," said Jane, brushing mud off Lana's dress. "Take my hand." But the remaining saloons all seemed even more menacing now than before, with their dimly lit doorways and noisy interiors. Jane looked heavenward for a moment at the constellations in a cloudless sky, and traced the bowl of the Big Dipper to the North Star, just as she had every clear night for months on the way to Bannack. That constant star still told her which way she faced, but it no longer gave her any clue of which way to go. Jane dropped her gaze to the street and saw a well-dressed man approaching. She wanted to run away rather than face a stranger in her present condition, but she walked towards him, swallowing her pride so hard it hurt. "Please, sir, can you help us find our Pa? My sister is hungry." She would have sooner chewed off her own arm than ask for help for herself.

The well-dressed stranger bent down to Jane's level, then turned to the man in the shadows with the long pigtail and indicated with a wave of his hand that he would take care of this.

"You must be Jane," he said, smiling.

"Yes, sir."

"It's late. Would you and your sister enjoy a meal with my family this evening?"

Tired, cold, hungry, wet and caked with mud, Jane looked at Lana, who gazed back at her with innocence and trust. "Thank you, mister. We would be much obliged," Jane said.

An hour or so later, Jane and Lana were warm and comfortable in the home of their hosts, Mr. and Mrs. Fergus, and their son Andrew, who was just about Jane's age. The girls had been scrubbed clean and provided with clothes acquired from neighbors. Mrs. Fergus carefully wrapped Jane's hand, blistered from the hot bean pot, in a clean, soft cloth. Girls' clothing was found for Lana, but for Jane only boys' clothing had been available. She felt kind of natural in a shirt and pants. The clothes were worn but patched neatly wherever needed, and a nice red bandana had been donated as well, which compensated for that hand-me-down look with a flair.

Jane discreetly surveyed the home of her hosts. This place was more comfortable than even their farm in Missouri had been. The Ferguses had an actual kerosene lamp, which lit the cabin so well that Jane could see into all its corners. There were cots for sleeping, and three-legged stools to sit on, and the whole place was clean, thanks in part to the cow-hides which covered the dirt floor. In one corner was a device that Jane guessed was a sewing machine by the way fabric and half-sewn clothing were arranged neatly around it. Everywhere were signs of order and comparative wealth.

Jane watched Mrs. Fergus cook a meal of bacon and biscuits with big eyes and a growling stomach. From time to time, Mrs. Fergus would wash her hands and wipe them on a large cloth sewn into a loop around a rod fixed to the wall. When Mrs. Fergus brought the girls each a full plate, Jane couldn't help but devour hers as if she hadn't seen a good meal like this in a week, because she hadn't.

The lamp light flickered on the boy Andrew's face as he watched Jane intently. She averted her gaze, wondering what he thought.

"You look like a boy," Andrew finally blurted.

Jane was relieved that Andrew hadn't said something much worse. Being called a tomboy didn't really bother her, but she felt she had to defend herself anyway. She wiped her mouth with her sleeve, ignoring the cloth napkin Mrs. Fergus had placed on the table in front of her.

"I'm more girl than you can handle," she replied.

Mrs. Fergus rolled her eyes, and Mr. Fergus let out half a chuckle, but the remark seemed to go over Andrew's head.

"Let's try to be a bit more lady-like, dear," Mrs. Fergus said primly. "Now, girls, it's time for all of us to go to bed."

A few minutes later, Lana slept at Jane's side on the floor, both wrapped in soft blankets. Lana's face was lit by a flickering candle, her corncob doll at her cheek. Jane was glad that Lana didn't seem to be embarrassed by their circumstances, but she sure was.

Jane fought sleep for a few minutes, remaining motionless, listening to her hosts with her head turned to the wall so they would think she was asleep.

"Those poor children," said Mr. Fergus. "I don't know what would have happened to them if the Chinaman hadn't found me."

"Where in the world are their parents, anyway?" Mrs. Fergus asked.

"Well, I'm told the father is a drunkard who is actually trying to make a living at gambling," Mr. Fergus said.

"How pathetic," said Mrs. Fergus. "And what about the mother?"

"The older one says she caught the typhoid," said Fergus.

"We can hope she recovers," said Mrs. Fergus. "She doesn't have enough sense to use well water?"

"That would be the least of her bad habits, I'm afraid," said Mr. Fergus.

"She's a drunkard, too?"

"Perhaps, but...how can I phrase this delicately?" Mr. Fergus said. "I'm afraid the woman has sunk to selling her favors, my dear."

"Those poor children," Mrs. Fergus said.

Jane felt as if a lead weight was pressing on her chest. So that's what all the whispering was about among their neighbors, the sidelong glances at the girls in the last few weeks. Ma had taken to prostitution. This was why the other parents kept their kids away from her and Lana. Anger fomented in Jane's mind as the Ferguses finished their preparations for bed: anger that she was an object of pity through no fault of her own.

The Ferguses blew out the last candle and settled into their own beds. In the quiet stillness, fatigue weighed heavier and heavier on Jane, until welcome sleep eased her tortured consciousness.

Chapter 2

Olaus Roemer, a Danish astronomer, had determined the speed of light almost two hundred years prior to these events by determining how the difference in the interval between successive eclipses of Jupiter's moons (by Jupiter itself) varied depending on whether the earth was moving towards Jupiter or away from it. One hundred eighty-six thousand miles per second: it is astonishing how gossip in a small town travels so close to that maximum speed. Not long after the sunrise that followed the girls' stay with the Ferguses, tongues were wagging all over Bannack about their predicament, at least among the womenfolk. Likewise the Ferguses learned that the wayward parents had returned home. Mrs. Fergus provided the girls with a hearty breakfast, and Jane helped her clean up afterwards. She furtively wrapped some scraps of food in a napkin as she did, which Mrs. Fergus pretended to not notice. When Mrs. Fergus bade them farewell, Jane thanked her, but had a hard time meeting her eyes. "Come, girls," said Mr. Fergus. Jane took Lana by the hand and followed her benefactor to the creek by a circuitous route around town, for even at this early hour occasional gunfire could be heard. Their goodbye at the bridge was made all the more awkward by Mr. Fergus' parting advice. "Maybe your Ma wouldn't have gotten sick if she had only taken well water," he said.

"I'll be sure to tell her that," said Jane.

Crossing the bridge was easy in the light of day, and Jane led Lana across by her hand, shuffling sideways quickly. Once across, they passed the gurgling sluices where men of tanned skin and muscular builds bantered and cursed as they shoveled gravel in one end, and at the other end sifted out the precious metal which had settled in the bottom of the wooden troughs. Proceeding up the gentle slope of the Salt Lake Road, they came to their neighborhood. Jane averted her eyes from a pair of mothers who gestured and sniffed in their direction.

Lana spotted her first. "Ma!" she cried as she dropped Jane's hand and ran for a joyous reunion.

"Oh, sweetie, are you all right?" Ma asked Lana as she weakly knelt and embraced her youngest. "Did Jane take good care of you?"

Jane tossed the table scraps to Queenie, who wagged her tail appreciatively.

"Someone is glad to see me, anyhow," she said, scowling at Ma. Prostitute. Whore, she thought.

"What happened to your hand?" asked Ma.

"Nothin'," said Jane.

"Don't you give me a look like that, young lady," Ma said.

"I got a right," Jane snapped.

"Really? What makes you think that?" Ma retorted. "I was sick."

"I heard things."

"What things?"

"Things."

Ma looked at the ground, then patted Lana's head. "It ain't like this town welcomed us with open arms when we got here, girl."

"So you decided to open your legs?" said Jane.

"You shut your mouth," Ma said.

Bob Canary came to the doorway, looking like he had been trampled by horses. "What's going on out here?" he asked. "And where did you get them clothes?"

"Across the creek," Jane replied.

"You look like a boy. Bandana's a nice touch, though."

"You look like three days of bad luck and worse whiskey," Jane shot back.

"You watch your mouth, young lady," Pa said. "Never mind them boys' clothes, you had damn well better act like a lady."

Jane glanced at Ma, who looked like she was avoiding Pa's gaze. Did Pa not know how un-ladylike Ma could be?

Charlotte Canary brushed Lana's hair with her hand. "We had a farm. Selling that about covered what it took to get here. Once we got here, we had to sell the oxen and the wagon for this miserable shack. Prices are so high out here... so next we had to sell the horse just so's we could eat." She looked Jane in the eye. "I do what I have to do."

Ma turned her back on Jane and reached for Lana. In the moment before Ma pulled Lana towards the cabin door, Jane saw her own anger reflected in her sister's face as an equal degree of hurt and pain.

"You'll be okay now, Lana," Jane choked. She hadn't thought of how the spatter of her own boiling emotions might scald her sister, and she blamed her parents all the more for that. An ache came to her throat, the one she felt when she put a lid on that pot boiling in her innards, an ache that made it that much harder to form words. If she didn't do something soon, her anger had a habit of exploding. Jane felt her face flush as she turned to Pa, who adjusted his shirt in an awkward, defensive kind of way.

Jane screwed up her face and dashed inside the cabin to the corner that cradled her squirrel gun. Her eyes could not see it well, but no matter, she knew where it was instinctively. On her way out, she patted

Queenie, whose puppies yipped at her ankles. "Soon you can come with me again, girl. Your puppies need

you," she said, loud enough. She stepped outside into the morning air, and felt the coolness of it soothe her throat. There stood Pa, shifting from one foot to the other without purpose. Anger melted into contempt. This was not the man who had taught her to use the squirrel gun now so comfortable in her grasp, taught her how to track larger game, how to read the earth and sky for survival. That was the man of her childhood. On the long dusty trail to Bannack, one night Indians stole some of the horses while that man was on sentry duty. The blame fell that much more harshly on him as some of the other men seemed to think that drink was partly to blame, and from that point the drinking only got worse. Now, the swaying, disheveled man before her was but a faint echo of the one who had taught her to use the gun in her bandaged left hand. Contempt faded to sadness.

"I'm going hunting," she said.

"I got eyes," said he.

Jane took a path away from town with a defiant stride. Away from the ever-toiling miners working the gravel of the creek in search of tiny specks of what the Indians called "the yellow metal that drives the white man crazy." Fifteen years old, won't be long before I can make my own way, Jane thought as she trod uphill in her new boots. Her long-barreled, .32 caliber muzzle-loader felt comforting in her grasp. Lana had her doll, she had this. She used the gun in her left hand to help her balance as she hiked uphill and found a rock to sit on. Thus situated, she counted out twenty grains of black gunpowder from her powder horn and fed them down the muzzle, then tamped in a lead ball carefully.

A twig snapped behind her, and Jane reflexively swung her gun towards the sound. There stood a wide-eyed Andrew Fergus, carrying a bundle of sticks.

"What the hell are you doing here?" demanded Jane as she lowered her weapon.

"Cuttin' stakes," was the reply. "And you have no cause to swear at me. Much less to shoot me."

"Sorry. I wasn't going to shoot you," she said.

"Coulda fooled me."

"I said I was sorry."

There was an awkward pause. "You catch it when you got home?" Andrew asked.

"Catch what?" Jane said. Andrew seemed nice enough. Not really her sort, though: he seemed a bit timid.

"You know. Catch...heck."

"Heck? You mean catch hell?" Jane asked. "Are you a Mormon or something, ain't supposed to swear?"

"No, we're agnostic."

"Agnostic. Never heard of that one." Jane prided herself on being as clever as anyone else she met, but her schooling had been sparse. "Agnostics don't swear?"

"Not as much as whatever you are."

"Never mind what I am," said Jane. "Queer mix of folk hereabouts. Are agnostic sermons really boring?"

"Ain't no agnostic church. It's a philosophy."

"So where do Agnostics go on Sunday?"

"It's not like that. Agnostic just means you figure that you don't know if there is a God or not," Andrew said.

"I thought that was what an atheist was."

"Nope. An atheist is sure there is no God."

"Oh," she said. "No matter. "I ain't much of one for church anyhow."

"Whatcha huntin'?" asked Andrew.

"Rabbits. Grouse if I spot 'em."

Andrew perked up. "Lemme see your gun," he said.

Jane handed it over.

"I shot a few ducks back in the States myself," he said proudly, and handed the weapon back to Jane. "Used birdshot."

"I use bullets," Jane said. "Don't usually get close enough for birdshot."

"Mind if I come along?" he asked.

"Can't see why not," Jane responded, with feigned ambivalence. "Where in the States you from?"

"Minnesota. My Dad started a mill back there. Did okay for a while."

So they started up the sage-covered hill together.

"What are those for?" Jane pointed to the stakes.

Andrew's face brightened. "I sell them to the butcher. He sells all his beef on these."

"I seen that," said Jane. "How come he don't wrap the beef in paper?"

"Paper is scarce around here. My Pa can't even find enough to write his journal," said Andrew. "How long you been in Bannack?"

"Few weeks." What really intrigued Jane was that Andrew made money. "How much does the butcher pay you for those?"

"A dollar for the bundle."

Not bad, thought Jane. Prices were high in Bannack due to the expense of shipping anything hundreds of miles over rough, dangerous trails from Salt Lake City. A dollar wouldn't buy near what it would

have back in Missouri, but it wasn't chicken feed either. Andrew's standing went up a notch is Jane's estimation.

The two continued hiking up the gentle hill in search of game, comparing as they went stories of how each had fared on their months-long overland trips to Bannack, led by scouts who seemed as wise in the ways of the wilderness as they were brave. Jane told of a perilous time when the ropes had slipped as their party lowered a wagon down a cliff, and Andrew told of being almost swept away crossing a swollen river. Like little kids, they competed as to who lost more livestock to Indian raids, who saw the bigger herds of buffalo, and so forth.

The pair climbed to a vantage point where Bannack could be seen in its entirety. The browned hills across the way looked like a row of pillows, nestling the creek that meandered at their feet. The town itself was a muddy smudge in this picture, a jumble of unpainted log structures, strewn unevenly at the lowest point in the otherwise scenic tableau. This smudge, marred further by smoke from dozens of tin chimneys, was divided unevenly by the creek. A dozen or so rustic homes, capped mostly by sod roofs, were on the near side of the creek, the Canary home no more or less prominent among them. The only substantial structure on this side was the octagonal "roundhouse", a solid fort-like structure that was large enough shelter for several families, which had been built by early arrivals as a refuge in case of Indian attack. Across the creek lay the bulk of the town, the mercantile section along Main Street, and in the hollow just beyond that, the orderly homes of those early arrivals to the goldfields like the Ferguses. Andrew pointed out the butcher shop whose proprietor paid him for his stakes. Attached to that was a pigpen, where hogs ate what little the butcher felt was not fit to be ground into sausage.

"See that there saloon on the corner with the tiger on the sign?" asked Jane.

"Sure."

"I been inside that one, just before I came to your place. Chinese couple runs it," said Jane.

The view from this vantage point was much like the first glimpse Jane had had of Bannack. Their wagon train had labored up the last hill and paused at the crest for that first look. Jane could see the disappointment in her parents' eyes and that of the other adults as they surveyed the ramshackle collection of buildings that made up Bannack. Not so for Jane, who had been excited by the possibilities of the place at first sight. She had decided then and there she was never going back to the tedious life of a remote farm in Missouri.

"It's a sight from up here, ain't it?" she asked Andrew.

"Yup," he said.

The pair continued uphill a ways. Jane was enjoying Andrew's company, but at the same time trying not to let on. It didn't take her long to spot a rabbit once she came to her favorite hunting spot.

"See 'im?" she said.

"Sure," said Andrew.

"That's dinner," she said as she drew the rifle to her shoulder.

"You ain't gonna waste lead from here?" Andrew asked.

Jane took aim and squeezed the trigger. There was a loud bang, a cloud of blue smoke, and the rabbit fell. "Ain't prone to waste bullets, myself," she replied.

"No way!" her companion said.

"Ain't so much," she said with a casual toss of her head. "I prob'ly coulda hit that rabbit from a horse at a trot." Maybe she was exaggerating, but not by much. She had a knack for marksmanship, a skill honed on the trip overland.

"Wow," said Andrew as they approached their fallen quarry. "You wanna meet my friends?"

"What friends?"

"The other kids."

Jane was warming up to Andrew, but she was reluctant to meet these other kids. What reception would they give a whore's daughter? "I should be going home," she said, fastening the rabbit to her belt with a leather thong.

"Aw, come on!" Andrew said. "You'll like them."

So with the rabbit bouncing against her thigh, Jane followed Andrew downhill towards town, past her home, past the miners working babbling streams in their sluices, to the double log bridge, which they crossed and headed upstream, away from town.

"The little kids call this Flower Canyon," said Andrew. "Everybody's parents let them come here 'cause it's safe."

They proceeded uphill to the canyon, where lush growth of greenery, berries, and flowers asserted nature's sovereignty over a stump-filled clearing. Close at hand was a group of girls gathering up flowers; more distant were two boys chopping wood and loading it into a wagon. A sway-backed horse hitched to the wagon waited patiently for them to finish.

The girls were mostly youngsters of Lana's age, one older girl supervising. "That's Dez," said Andrew. "I don't know why they call her that, all her boyfriends. Her real name is Matilda, but she likes her friends to call her Dez. Hey, Dez."

"Hey, Andrew," replied the older girl as they drew closer.

"Do you know Jane?" Andrew asked.

"Never met," said Dez. She was a truly beautiful young woman of about seventeen, aloof and self-assured, and she had a feminine presence which made Jane feel a little awkward and aware of her tomboy appearance.

"Pleased to meet you," said Jane. "Whatcha doin'?"

"Babysitting," said Dez. "I don't mind. Pay's okay."

One of the younger girls held up her bouquet. "We sell flowers to the saloons!" she said.

"And greens to the store!" chimed another girl, holding up her basket for Jane to see.

Jane compared this freshly scrubbed cherub in her nice dress to Lana, and felt a pang of embarrassment. "Those are pretty," she said.

Jane and Andrew proceeded towards the boys, who worked on a dead-fall tree with an axe. "Your family favor the North or the South?" said Andrew.

"North," said Jane.

"Us, too," said Andrew. "These two are the Kirkpatrick brothers. Their folks favor the South. Hey, guys."

The boys paused at their work and regarded Jane and her squirrel gun.

"Who's this?" the older brother asked Andrew.

"Name's Jane," she said.

"I'm James." The younger boy pointed to the rabbit. "That your dinner?"

"Looks like it."

"You shoot it?" asked the older boy.

"She shot it from musta been forty yards," Andrew interjected for his new friend.

"All the girls shoot good where you're from?" asked James.

"Naw, mostly just me," Jane said.

The older boy scowled and spit. "You look funny in my old duds."

So that's where the Ferguses got my clothes, thought Jane.

"Still look like a whore's spawn," the older boy continued.

"Take it back," Jane said.

"Which part, that you look funny or that your Ma is a drunken whore?" he asked. "And by the way, yer Pa is a lousy card cheat."

"I'm giving you one more chance. Take it back." Jane felt anger well up in her. Her throat was in a knot, and she felt flushed.

"You are giving me one more chance, eh? That's a laugh. Look at her in that outfit," he said to Dez. "You got…"

Jane snapped. While Robert was looking at Dez, she tackled him, knocking him to the ground. The older boy's words were swallowed mid-sentence as Jane set on him like a badger, cuffing and kicking him in a fury. "Ow, dammit, you know I can't hit no girl," said the older boy as he pushed her away. "No fair."

The younger girls screamed, but Jane didn't stop, and the older boy had to absorb, blow by blow, all Jane's pent-up anger: the anger and frustration that had built up from the moment that the clump of dirt fell into the pot to the moment she walked out of her home without calling her Ma a whore.

Dez came to the boy's rescue, pulling Jane off him, and Andrew stepped between them.

Jane dusted off and took a step back. "You should be more polite, like your brother," she said to the older boy.

"You are a calamity," said the older boy. "That's what they call you now, you know. Calamity Jane."

"I'll be your personal calamity any day of the week, I reckon," she said. She lunged at Robert one more time, but Andrew blocked her way. Her red bandana had come off in the tussle, and lay in the dirt. Jane picked it up. "Here, ya jerk, you can have this." Robert caught the tossed cloth, crumpled and dirty, and stuffed it in his pocket with a scowl.

"By the way, don't know as if I caught your name," said Jane.

"Robert, if you have to know," he said. "Come on, James, let's haul this load home." He took off his leather gloves and carefully tucked them in his shirt. The boys climbed on their wagon, and Robert flicked the reins, driving the horse towards town.

Andrew stood by Jane as the brothers departed. "You got a temper," he said.

"Yeah, I heard that one before," said Jane.

"Robert's okay, really, once you get to know him."

"I know him as much as I care to already," said Jane.

"Come on, girls," said Dez to the little ones. "Time to go home." She gathered the girls to her. "You got a problem, girl," she said. "Sort it out." In a huff, she headed towards town.

"So long, then," said Andrew.

"Yeah," said Jane, wondering if she would ever see him again, and cursing her own bad temper silently.

Chapter 3

The next day when Jane rose from her buffalo-hide bed, Ma was already cooking biscuits and beans over the sheet-iron stove. "Come and get it," she said.

Jane sized up breakfast and calculated how much she could eat and still leave enough for Lana. She took just that portion on a plate and started scooping up beans with her biscuit.

"There's a fork over there, you know," said Ma with half a scowl.

"Don't have no use for it," Jane answered.

Jane ate her food silently, peering at Ma all along. Seemed a bit subdued this morning.

"You don't have to look at me like that," said Ma.

"I ain't looking at you like nothin'," said Jane.

"I told you, I do what I have to do. Things stay like this, well, all we got left to sell is the stove."

"Does Pa know?"

"Now he does," Ma said, with a sidelong glance.

"I'm going," Jane said.

"Stay away from town. Could be trouble."

"Why?"

"It's the Fourth of July."

"What kind of trouble?" asked Jane.

"You know. The war."

Sure, she knew about the war. Everybody did. If a Northerner wanted to clarify which side they took, they would call it "The Great Rebellion." If someone was from the South, they called it "The War of Northern Aggression." At every major stop on the Canary's trek West, men of better education had read newspaper accounts aloud to little groups, with Jane listening in as often as she could. These newspaper reports detailed great battles in faraway places Jane had never heard of before, with thousands of men killed. To her, it all seemed so remote that the war could just as well have been fought on the moon. However, many men in Bannack had fought in those battles, and either been discharged, injured, or deserted; they tended to still take that faraway conflict quite personally. Greaseball from Madam Chi's was not the only man in town who wore the remnants of a uniform.

"Secesh is likely to take exception to any Yankee celebration," Ma said. "And they's way more Secesh than Yankees hereabouts." They didn't like being called "Secesh", either.

"Slavery is an abomination in the sight of God." Pa was out of bed now, scratching and stretching as he spoke.

Jane had heard this from Pa often enough that it didn't usually deserve comment, but today she was still in a cranky mood. "How come you didn't join the army anyhow?" she asked.

"Got a family to feed, you know. I would think you could see that," he said.

"And a fine job you are doing," muttered Jane, barely loud enough for her to hear herself.

"What did you say?" asked Pa. "What was that?"

"Nothin'." She finished her food and wiped her hands on her pants. Boys' clothing was so much more practical than flimsy girls' attire. Pa cast her a scowl and retired inside.

"Secesh don't scare me none, anyhow," Jane said to Ma.

"Don't want you to come in no crossfire," said Ma.

"Could just as well catch a bullet here as there," said Jane. "Can't stay inside all day."

"Go then."

An advantage of having neglectful parents was that they did not encumber Jane with many restrictions. "I'll be home for supper," she said as she glanced to see that her squirrel gun was carefully propped in its corner. She bent down and scratched Queenie behind the ears, then picked up a puppy, who licked her face.

"Don't get too attached to them puppies," Ma told Jane as she headed out the door. "I promised the pick of the litter to Dr. Glick, and the rest to others that we owe."

Jane skipped past the sluices, only a few of which were being worked today. She wondered why any miners were working at all on a holiday, but when she heard German spoken in one claim and another language she didn't recognize further on, she figured she knew why. A huge black man paused from shoveling gravel into a sluice and their eyes met for a moment. Jane had barely ever seen blacks back home, but here among men drawn from all over the world, he barely deserved notice.

Jane skipped across the bridge and was about to head toward town when she noticed Andrew in the meadow up in Flower Canyon. Not sure of the footing on which they had parted, she waved. He waved back, so she headed in his direction.

"Hey," she greeted him.

"Hey. How's your temper today?"

"I'm fine, long's nobody picks a fight," she said gruffly.

"I ain't gonna pick a fight with you," Andrew said defensively.

"Wasn't talking about you," Jane said quickly. She hadn't meant to offend.

"Where you going?" Andrew asked.

"It's the Fourth," she said. "Just out to see what's goin' on."

"You got any fireworks?" Andrew asked.

"No. Where would I get those?" Jane was relieved that Andrew still seemed friendly.

"Chinaman sells 'em. Name's Lo. Won Hung Lo they call him."

"Who calls him that?"

"Everybody. It's a joke. Nobody knows his real first name, so they call him that, 'cuz..."

"I get the joke. You gonna buy fireworks?"

"Naw."

"Why not? You spend all your money?"

"Naw. It's just I'm not allowed closer to town than this."

"Really?" asked Jane. "I could buy some for you."

Andrew's face brightened for a moment, and then hesitation crossed it.

"What?" asked Jane.

"What I want to buy costs a lot."

It took a moment to guess the reason for Andrew's hesitation. "Don't worry none. My Ma's a whore, my Pa's a poor excuse for a card sharp, but they taught me to starve rather than steal. Your money is safe with me, Andrew."

"Don't get riled, there. I don't care to mess with you when you get riled."

"I ain't going to get riled at a friend." She watched him to see how he would take that, the label of friend. "Go get your money—let's buy you some fireworks."

So Andrew trotted home, and in short order returned with a small bundle clutched in his hand. "Should be ten dollars here," he panted. He unwrapped a glass inkwell from a cloth.

Jane took the inkwell carefully from him. Though it was rare that anything in Bannack was purchased except with gold wrested from the creek, she had never had actual gold in her possession before, or anything near ten dollars in any form. She grasped the inkwell tightly. "Don't worry—I'll get you ten dollars' worth of fireworks." She stuck out her hand, and they shook on the agreement.

So Jane headed towards town, caution in her stride. When she came to Main Street, she gave a wide berth to Skinner's with the fancy double row of glass panes on either side of the door and its false front. It was funny how the most dangerous establishment in town presented the biggest and fanciest false front, Jane thought. Soon she was at the threshold of Madam Chi's. Seeing it in daylight, it seemed so much more flimsy than the other saloons, and isolated from the rest. She pushed open the door. Before her eyes could adjust, a man bellowed, "Madam Chi!" from a gambling table. The rustling of a silk skirt announced the presence of the proprietress.

"May I help you, my dear?" said Chi.

"I have business with Lo," Jane said, trying to sound as if she did this every day.

"What business? All business here my business," said Chi.

Burning incense sticks wafted their essence into the atmosphere. So that's where that spice smell came from, thought Jane. "I want to buy firecrackers," she said. Chi beckoned her to a back storeroom with a brusque gesture. There, Lo was busy pouring whiskey from a wooden keg into a glass decanter.

"Girl need firecrackers. You have more?" Chi asked.

Lo waved Chi away with a dismissive flick of his hand. Turning to Jane, his smile became sly but friendly. "Miss Calamity," he said as he bowed.

"Yeah, I learned that's my nickname," said Jane. "You got one, too, I hear."

" 'Won Hung Lo,' " he said. "They honor me more than they know with this name. This mean I have balls. You know 'balls'?" he asked.

"Sure, I know 'balls,' " Jane said.

Lo laughed. "You want see firecrackers?"

He pulled a box from an upper shelf. As he did, the loose sleeve on his silk shirt fell back and Jane saw a tattoo on his forearm. She had never seen one like it before; it was an eye with lines radiating from it, as if it could see in all directions. Lo saw her curiosity. "I tell you story sometime," was all he said, as he swung the box down from the shelf and his sleeve fell to cover the tattoo.

Jane thrust the inkwell to Lo. "How much can I buy for ten dollars' worth of dust?"

Lo directed Jane to a table where he poured the gold into a small, thin dish that he had placed on piece of thick paper.

"You be careful with gold," said Lo.

"Gotta be careful," said Jane, "it ain't mine."

"Someday, you have gold. You watch out when buy with gold," said Lo. "See here, paper under bowl. I spill, just pour from paper into bowl."

"Easier, I guess," said Jane.

"Easy, yes," said Lo, "But easy not important. You watch out. Other man put dish on carpet. He spill,

you lose gold in carpet. Months come, go, man burn carpet, keep gold."

"Thanks," said Jane. "One way to tell who's honest around here, huh?"

Lo produced a handheld scale and placed a weight on one side and the dish on the other. "Ten

dollar?" he asked, after examining it closely. "Ten dollar fifty good price."

Jane pursed her lips and squinted at the gold, speckled with black sand grains. "Done," she said.

Lo pulled a leather pouch out from somewhere under his silken garments, and poured the dust into the pouch without spilling a single flake.

Outside, Jane heard a commotion: men shouting and gunshots.

"Ten dollar fifty buy these," said Lo, holding up a big string of firecrackers, each individually smaller than her little finger. "No big firecrackers blow off girl's fingers."

Lo wrapped the firecrackers with a string and handed them to Jane.

"Thank you, Mr. Lo," she said, tucking the little bundle under her arm.

"Missy Calamity," said Lo. He bowed slightly to Jane, who bowed as well, took a step backwards, then turned and left the backroom. She passed the gaming tables with their neat stacks of poker chips and the men hunched around them, and headed to the door. She pushed past several men who loitered there, watching the commotion outside.

Jane couldn't see much at first as her eyes adjusted to sunlight again. She proceeded slowly so as to not trip in the wagon ruts, as she had the last time she left Madam Chi's. She could make out a crowd of men outside Skinner's saloon in one direction. Opposing them were a handful of men who seemed to be engaged in some sort of construction. As soon as her eyes adjusted enough, Jane ran around the men, back to Andrew up in Flower Canyon.

"Got 'em!" she said as she unwrapped the bundle.

Andrew had a stick with a smoking ember at one end, and soon the friends were having great fun unraveling the string of firecrackers, lighting and throwing them. They tired of that soon, though, and began blowing up discarded oyster tins and such that they found lying about. They did not notice in their excitement that their hunt for such objects had brought them closer and closer to town, until they crested a little ridge and found themselves within a few yards of the men from Skinner's saloon. The shouting had stopped, and the situation had turned quite tense. The two groups were in a muttering face-off.

"My Dad!" said Andrew.

There he was, indeed, at the head of a small group of men. They had dug a hole in the ground and placed one end of a long pole near it. Two men supported the pole midway, and a thirty-five star U.S. flag fluttered on the very end. The men who had emptied from Skinner's saloon greatly outnumbered these half-dozen Yankees, whose resolve at this moment was wavering.

Mr. Fergus addressed his compatriots. "Men, pay no attention to these scowling wretches. We have nothing to fear from men who have run fifteen hundred miles to avoid a fight!"

"My Dad's in trouble—look!" Andrew whispered to Jane. Among the Secesh was Greaseball, the leering sleazebag she had first encountered at Madam Chi's. Still attired in that tattered gray uniform, he was loading his gun, muttering and snarling at Mr. Fergus between loads.

Jane grabbed the ember stick and firecrackers before Andrew could protest. She lit the entire string of remaining firecrackers and threw them behind Greaseball. The fireworks went off in their characteristic staccato rhythm, causing Greaseball to turn towards the noise with alarm and confusion. Several other Secesh turned as well, guns drawn and ready. Andrew froze.

"Come on!" said Jane, taking the view that a strategic retreat was in their best interest. She grabbed Andrew's arm and led him in the opposite direction with a sharp pull, and they both ran as quickly as they could. The Secesh were chagrined to see that they had momentarily confused firecrackers for gunfire, but they were not inclined to make themselves look more foolish by giving chase to children. Mr. Fergus, seizing the initiative, ordered the flag pole raised, which was done, and wooden shims were pounded alongside the pole to secure it.

There were curses shouted by the Secesh, and epithets such as "Lincoln-lovers" and, more grating on Jane's ears, "nigger lovers"; but the Yankees ignored this as they saluted their flag. Mr. Fergus led them in singing "The Battle Hymn of the Republic", oblivious of the role his son had played in his success at raising Old Glory.

Jane and Andrew did not look back as they made a clean getaway, running and laughing all the way to the safety of Flower Canyon. The last thing Jane saw as she looked back was Greaseball giving her a dirty look.

Chapter 4

So tell me, what was your name in the States?
Was it Johnson or Thompson or Bates?
Did you murder your wife?
Did you flee for your life?
So tell me, what was your name in the States?
—Contemporary ditty

The canvas door flaps of the Canary home twisted lazily in the breeze, causing shards of light from a late afternoon sun to dance gently on the dirt floor.

"Come on now, Jane. I told Doctor Glick you would bring the puppy to him today," Ma said. "You've dawdled long enough."

Charlotte had really mended her ways in the last few weeks. She didn't care so much about the gossip, but when Lana had started asking questions that she didn't really want to answer, she had sobered up, and as far as Jane could tell, ceased her illicit sexual exploits. Ma now took in laundry to make money. This appeared to be a much less lucrative enterprise than prostitution as far as Jane could see, however, as the family seemed to be in more dire financial straits than ever.

"You be respectful to the doctor, Jane," Ma said.

"Long's he don't treat me like I got some disease, we'll get along fine." Jane scooped up the squiggly little puppy in her arms and cuddled him while he licked her face.

"You act respectful, however he treats you," said Ma.

It grated on Jane to take lessons in propriety from such a fallen angel as Ma, but she held her tongue. Lana ran over to say goodbye to the puppy, and giggled as he licked her face as well. Then Jane was off for Dr. Glick's. She didn't know much about him other than that he rode a magnificent white stallion with an ornate Mexican saddle and silver stirrups around town, and he lived on a small ranch just over the hill on the road to Salt Lake City.

Jane walked slowly, allowing the puppy to follow her along the path, stopping to sniff and investigate whatever aroused his curiosity, which seemed to be nearly everything. He brought Jane a stick and dropped it at her feet, so she gave it a little toss. The puppy caught on to the "fetch" game pretty quickly for such a

youngster, so Jane tested him by tossing the stick farther and farther away as they proceeded down the path to the Salt Lake City Road.

Upon reaching the road, Jane heard the rumble of a big supply wagon coming over the hill. It was mostly Mormons who drove wagons north on the road from Salt Lake City to Bannack. They were sturdy, industrious, and wily. Pa dismissed them as a bunch of bigamists, but they were the town's lifeline for supplies, and they were always polite to Jane. She scooped up the puppy as the wagon approached.

Something was wrong. The full-bearded driver met her gaze without changing his grim expression. The wagon came closer, and she saw blood on his coat. As the wagon passed, through the cloud of dust came a sight that knotted Jane's stomach. The limp form of a man bounced like a rag doll. The wagon forded the creek and the driver reined in his team of oxen in front of the dry goods store. Jane followed, carrying the puppy in her arms across the bridge.

Little notice was taken when one rough shot another in a barroom brawl, but this was different. A shout went out that a man had been killed. Miners put down their shovels, and townsfolk out on errands gathered as well. Mr. Fergus had been engaged in conversation with friends in the street and was one of the first to the wagon.

"They got us a couple miles back," said the Mormon. "My partner winged one of them so this is what they did to him."

A well-dressed man wearing dapper gambler's garb inspected the body. "You recognize any of them?" he asked.

"No—they had flour bags for masks and their horses were covered," the Mormon replied.

Men exited Skinner's and lounged with skeptical demeanor.

"We might catch them if we head out now," said Fergus.

"Who we got that can track 'em?" asked one of his friends.

"Can't be hard. One's wounded.," said Fergus.

"What have you boys ever tracked before?" asked the man dressed in the fine suit.

There was an agitated silence.

"Nothing, then?" he asked.

"You don't look like the tracker type yourself, mister. Who are you to say?" asked someone.

"Name's Plummer, for those of you that don't know me. Henry Plummer. Was Sheriff back in California, and I've done my share of manhunts." Plummer was confident and fearless in his manner, and reminded Jane of her favorite scout with his lean, athletic build.

"Then let's go," said one of Fergus' friends. "I'll get the rope."

"Now hold on," said Plummer. "I will lead you in pursuit of the villains who did this, but not down the path of anarchy. If I am leading this operation, then we bring the suspects back here for a trial."

"Trial, hell," said another. "Ain't no law out here. Leastwise you to tell us what to do."

"Now I understand how you all feel," said Plummer, "but I suggest that we, the good citizens of this newborn community, should take no steps that would bring disgrace on our rising city."

"A man's been killed!" said another.

"And let's not make things worse by vigilante justice," said Plummer.

That little speech threw cold water on the affair, and men who were poised for action like coiled springs moments before now shuffled their feet. It was obvious to Jane that nobody was going to give chase.

Seemed a shame to her that they wouldn't follow this Plummer fellow. The puppy squirmed in Jane's arms, so as the little crowd dispersed, she returned across the footbridge to finish her errand.

She proceeded on the Salt Lake City Road and soon crested the hill. In the little hollow was a cabin, and a man outside washing some bloody cloths. Wasn't much question who this was, nor whose blood he washed. She hugged the puppy and closed the gap between her and Glick.

"You must be Jane," he said. "It's good you didn't come earlier."

"Maybe I coulda helped."

Glick raised his eyebrows, then a smile crossed his face. "Maybe so," he said.

"Was he dead when he got here?" she asked.

"Not quite, but I'm afraid there was nothing I could do."

"They was going to chase the ones that done it back in town, but then they went and talked themselves out of it," said Jane. "I brung the puppy."

Glick picked up the puppy, which wagged its tail and yipped.

"What's his name?"

"We didn't name him. But he's a damn good fetcher for a puppy."

"Really?" said Glick. "Maybe I should name him Fetch."

"Naw, don't do that. Then he can't tell if you are calling him or telling him what to do."

"Now that would be a canine conundrum," Glick said, with a laugh. "Then how about Lucky? That's a good name for a dog in these parts."

"Why don't you name him Fetch and then just call him by the nickname Lucky?" Jane asked.

Glick smiled, squinting. "Well said, Calamity Jane. Everyone around here seems to need a nickname. Y'all want to know what nickname they have given me?"

Jane shrugged a silent "yes."

"The Yankees call me the Secesh Grapevine Telegraph," he said, "because I am the one that reads the Southern boys the New York newspaper when it comes to town."

Jane liked Glick. He didn't treat her so like a kid. "That's a catchy one, Dr. Secesh Grapevine Telegraph."

"Not as succinct as 'Calamity Jane', I suppose," said Glick. "How is your mother's health?"

"Seems good enough."

"You don't seem so pleased with her good health."

"I'm grateful to you for curing her," Jane said.

"And your Pa?" he asked.

"Drunk or hung over, one or the other pretty much all the time," replied Jane.

"I understand he used to be a very different man," Glick said.

Jane thought of her years on the farm, how Pa had taught her to hunt and ride. "Yeah," was all she said.

"Everybody has their flaws and imperfections, my dear," Glick said softly. "I could tell you all sorts of tales of the kinds of flaws and imperfections that land a man out here. I know a man who lost everything when a battlefield engulfed his home back in Virginia. Southern sympathizer, lost his home, his family. He was so angry that he headed to Colorado and got caught up in a raid on a Union supply train. The gang he had fallen in with got caught and he was thrown in jail. He'd still be there, but some other Secesh—you call them Secesh, right? They broke him out of jail."

"Really?" asked Jane. "Then what happened?"

"Oh, he's practicing his profession here," said Glick. "And everybody thinks he's an upstanding citizen. So all I'm saying is that you can't hardly find anyone here that is squeaky clean."

Throughout this conversation, Jane showed what a great fetcher Lucky was, until the puppy tuckered out, curled up in a ball, and went to sleep. Without the distraction of Lucky, Jane became aware of the time.

"I should be getting home," she said.

"Let me be a good host and cook y'all a good meal," said Glick.

"Y'all" is such an endearing term; that combined with her growling stomach convinced Jane to accept the invitation. Glick prepared a meal of choice steak, bread and butter, delicious raisins, and a salad of greens; lambsquarters, turns out they were called, which he pointed out had been picked by her little friends in Flower Canyon.

"You don't want to get scurvy, Jane," he said as he dished the greens. Conversation over dinner was light-hearted, and Jane was thoroughly enjoying herself mid-meal when horses approached outside. Glick went to the door and peered into the waning light. He stiffened and hurried back to her.

"How are you at the sight of blood?"

"Don't bother me none," Jane said.

Two rough-looking men burst through the door and aided an injured third man inside. Little was said

between any of them as the injured man was aided into a chair at the table, still cluttered with their half-eaten meal. The men seemed to be familiar with Glick, and he with them. It was the injured man who took note of Jane first.

"Who is this?" he asked.

"This is Jane, my nurse," Glick said.

"Nurse! That's a girl?"

Her tomboy clothes felt so natural to Jane that she had forgotten how strangers might see her.

"Jane is an excellent nurse," said Glick.

One of the two who had aided the other into the chair regarded Jane suspiciously. "Jane. Jane. Hmm. You wouldn't be Calamity Jane, would you?"

Jane didn't like the looks of this one at all. Rough, aggressive manners and the face of a weasel. "There's some what calls me that," she said.

"Jane who?" asked the third man: a big, burly fellow, with one blind, glassy-looking eye that he hadn't had the sense to put a patch over.

"Never you mind," Weasel-Snout snorted. "You go watch the door."

Glass-Eye shuffled to a sentry post at the door.

"So this is the unfortunate Calamity Jane," said Weasel-Snout. "Well, any friend of yours is a friend of ours, Doc."

"In my view, ours is a purely professional relationship," Glick returned icily.

So they did know each other, Jane thought. And obviously, these were the men who had robbed the Mormon and murdered his partner.

Glick turned to the injured man and picked up his swollen arm by the thumb, peering all around it. A bullet hole was apparent at the elbow, and the forearm was a mottled purple, swollen to about twice normal size. Glick glanced at Jane to see how the sight of blood and gore was affecting her. She caught this look and just shrugged. Glick nodded and gave her a little smile.

"This is as bad as it looks," Glick said. "Bullet went in here, but there is no exit wound. No telling where the bullet is in there." He gently set the arm back down on the table and cleared their half-finished meal. He opened a wooden instrument case, which the injured bandit regarded from the corner of his eye. The fine-toothed saw in that kit got Jane's attention. Glick drew a small bottle of liquid from the case. "You'll need a good dose of this," he said, holding it up.

The man shook his head. "None of that, Doc," he said. "I seen a man croak from that stuff. But I

could sure use some whiskey."

"Whiskey is a poor substitute for laudanum."

"I'll be still as a statue, Doc," said the injured man. "That's all you need, right?"

Glick shrugged and pointed to a bottle behind Weasel-Snout. "Give him that, then," he said.

Weasel-Snout fetched it, pulled the cork with his teeth, and handed the bottle to the injured man, who took a large swig and handed it back.

"Keep that handy," he told his partner.

"Jane, would you please take your usual position?" Glick asked, motioning to his side.

"Sure, Doc," she said.

"Clean all the dried blood off." He gave her a wet towel as he held the injured arm up by the thumb again.

The injured man winced and looked at Jane skeptically as she dabbed and rubbed the dried blood away. He must suspect that she had never done this before, she thought.

"Looks bad," she said to Glick, as though she could remember a dozen similar cases to compare to this one.

"No shit, girlie," Weasel-Snout said.

Glick paused in his preparations. He set the arm down on a clean cloth, and turned to Weasel-Snout. "This is going to be a delicate procedure, my good man. I'm sure y'all are aware."

"Sure, Doc, but you can do it."

"I'll do my best," Glick replied. "I have but one requirement of you. There is no reason for you to assault this youngster's ears with foul language, and I will not stand for it." He paused. "Do we understand each other?"

"Like she ain't heard worse where she come from," said Weasel-Snout.

"Dammit, be nice to her," said the injured man. "She's my nurse."

"You had better just do your job, Doc," said Weasel-Snout.

"I'll do my job, don't you worry. By the way, where is your boss this evening?"

"Never you mind about him," said Weasel-Snout. "I'm the one you take orders from now."

"Let him do his goddamn job," said the injured bandit. "It ain't you he's going to be poking around in. I want my doctor to be thinking right when he has a knife halfway through my arm. Doc," he said, "let's get down to business."

"Indeed," said Glick, turning his attention to the arm again. "Excellent job, Jane. Now we begin." He again picked up the arm by the thumb with one hand and gently felt with the other ("palpated," he explained) the length and circumference of the forearm for the bullet.

"Do you remember what position your arm was in when you were shot?" asked Glick.

"There was lots goin' on at the time," the bandit replied.

"No matter. It's just that it might give me a clue where to look if you did remember."

"There was a lot goin' on at the time," said the bandit.

Glick picked and probed, and as he did, described to Jane what he was doing. He removed dead muscle ("devitalized tissue," he said) with a knife ("scalpel") and spicules of bone with tweezers ("forceps"). He taught her the names of the nerves (radial, median, and ulnar) as he tested whether the bandit could sense a bit of cloth brushed against his skin. He showed Jane how to test blood flow in the arm by having the patient make a fist while compressing both the radial artery at the thumb side of the wrist and the opposite ulnar artery, then releasing one artery at a time to see if the hand "pinked up."

"If he loses circulation, I will have to open up your patient's arm from here to here to relieve the pressure," he said, indicating the entire length of the forearm.

Jane swelled with pride when Glick referred to this tough guy as "your patient"—as if he was her personal responsibility. She was doubly proud when Glick praised her for how quickly she learned the names of instruments and anatomy. Even the bandits seemed grudgingly impressed.

The probing and picking proceeded monotonously, with Jane alternately holding the arm in position or handing Glick instruments. As time wore on, Glick said less and less, and a frown seemed to permanently take root on his previously impassive face. He seemed to Jane to be perplexed that he could not find the bullet, and became more so as minutes piled up into an hour and more.

Much as Glick progressively showed more and more frustration, the patient showed more and more distress, despite repeated doses of the whiskey provided by Weasel-Snout. He gritted his teeth silently, sweat pouring off his brow. The arm had swollen even more over the course of Glick's probing and manipulation, and now the injured man could barely move the fingers of the affected arm. The operation was not going well.

Time wore close to two hours. Jane's back ached from standing, but she didn't dare sit. Dull-witted Glass-Eye, still standing sentry at the door, yawned and stretched, and Weasel-Snout fidgeted. Glick finally pushed back and shook his head. He sighed, then addressed the patient. "I'm afraid that your best hope is to be buried with this bullet, some day long from now, because I cannot remove it. The worst case is that this comes to amputation in the next few days. In either case you probably ought to get used to the idea of being a lefty."

"Won't be no amputation, Doc," slurred the now inebriated bandit. "I'm a dead man without it for sure, so one way or another, I'll go to my grave in one piece."

"We can hope that we don't have to make that choice," Glick said. He wrapped the wound in a clean dressing ("but not constricting," he told Jane) and gave instructions to Weasel-Snout on keeping the arm elevated and what to watch for that would require the patient to return. "Usually I would make a house call tomorrow," he said, "but given the circumstances, I will just leave y'all an open invitation to return."

The injured bandit rose and stumbled towards the door. Weasel-Snout reached into his coat and tossed a leather pouch on the table. "A small token of our thanks, Doc," he said.

"Keep it," Glick snapped. "That's the Mormon's money, and I can't give it back to his partner without revealing your guilt."

"Very well," said Weasel-Snout. "Just remember what you been told before. If word ever gets out about this, then you are a dead man."

"And you should keep in mind the saying 'he who lives by the sword, dies by the sword'," said Glick. "And if not by the sword, then certainly by the noose."

Weasel-Snout glared at Glick and snatched the pouch off the table.

"What about her?" asked Glass-Eye.

Jane felt Weasel-Snout's cold-hearted stare for a moment.

"She seems like a smart girl who would know what's best for her and the good doctor," he said. "But you are right. I suppose I should make myself more clear." He crouched down to below Jane's height, and put his face uncomfortably close to hers. “No one would miss you much, Calamity darlin’. Just keep that in mind.”

Jane took a deep breath. “Jerk,” she said. “Murderer.”

“If you want. Just keep it to yourself, ya whore’s daughter.” He turned to the other villains. “Whatya think boys, this ones kinda cute herself, huh?”

A mean laugh flickered on Weasel-Snout’s lips for only a moment before Jane’s boot caught him square in the crotch.

“You won’t be using that for a while. Name’s Jane to you. Calamity to my friends, but we ain’t friends.”

Weasel-Snout made a grab for her, but stumbled in pain. Glick stepped between the two.

“Get out, the lot of you, before I throw you out,” he said.

“You’re lucky I just ain’t the type to hit a girl,” said Weasel-Snout.

“Oh yeah, you’re a real gentleman, you are,” retorted Jane.

“Come on, Lefty,” said Weasel-Snout.

“Thanksh, Doc,” slurred newly-christened “Lefty”, as he went for the brim of his hat with his good hand and missed. “Calamity, if I may call you that. Damn good nurse.”

Without a further word the men left.

Chapter 5

When Jane returned home, Ma did not show any sign that she had been worried about her daughter's late return. Pa was off at the poker tables as usual.

"Puppy seems happy with Dr. Glick," was all Jane said.

"Get some sleep," said Ma. "Tomorrow is laundry day."

Jane was exhausted, so she willingly complied.

The bulk of Ma's new enterprise as a laundry woman was done on Saturdays, so that the miners would have clean clothes for their one day off on Sunday. Pa did some of the preparation, all the while grumbling that it was "squaw work." He carried water to be boiled, put up clothesline, started the outdoor fire for the big kettle, and hauled enough firewood for the day. Then he shaved, in order to look the part of card sharp, and set off for town. The bulk of the work was left for the women of the family. Jane went from customer to customer picking up men's clothing that reeked of sweat and grime turned rancid. She held her breath and wrapped each load in a sheet, then lugged it back home, where she dumped it on the ground. Ma would pick among these articles of clothing with a pole and toss them into the steaming wooden wash barrel. Periodically she would add hot water to the barrel from an iron kettle that hung on a tripod over the fire. Ma stirred and churned the clothes in the wash barrel, then transferred them to a rinse barrel with the pole, then to a clothes line. Lana was put to work as well, shaving a bar of lye soap into the wash barrel, and picking up smaller articles of clothes, usually with her nose pinched tight and her arm as outstretched it would go. As soon as Jane had dumped one load, she was off for the next. Travelling from claim to claim kept her hands busy, but her mind raced, churning the whole gory mess of events at Dr. Glick's like they were clothes in the barrel.

At one mining claim, she was greeted by the giant black man she had seen before. "You are Miss Calamity, aren't you?" he said, as Jane admired his bulging biceps.

"Sure am. What's your name?"

"Cecil. Cecil Jones. You work hard, don't you girl?" he said.

"Got to," she said.

"Me, too," he said, his smile widening.

"We'll get this laundry clean enough for you and your partners," she said.

"Ain't my partners. I work for these boys. But they treat me good."

Jane had never spoken to a black man before. "You escape your slave master?" she asked.

"No, Missy. I am a free man," he said. "Why Missy, you want to see my papers?" he teased.

"Keep 'em- I believe you. Why you come out here?"

"I was a white man's manservant, traveling on business. He went and killed another white man in a fight. Looked like they might come after me, so I ran. Kept running 'til I got to where the law don't reach. That's here, ain't it?"

"Sure seems like it is," she said.

"Well, I'll see you next Saturday, right Missy?"

"Sure, see ya 'round." Jane hoisted the bundle on her shoulder and headed home.

Back at the Canary cabin, laundry hung like haphazard fencing all around the cabin. Jane helped wash and hang this last load, and then took leave of Ma and Lana. She took the trail to the bridge, skipped across that, and headed to the Fergus' cabin. Her mind still jangled: could she tell Andrew anything of her stint as a nurse? She turned the events over and over in her mind as she rounded a corner and came to her destination. There she found Andrew helping Mr. Fergus put the finishing touches on a coffin. She stopped dead in her tracks.

"Good afternoon, Jane," Mr. Fergus said somberly. He pounded the last few nails without a word spoken by any of the three. "Sometimes I'm sorry I brought my family to this hellhole," he finally said.

"Can't say it's boring," Jane said.

Fergus placed the lid on the coffin to check its fit and gave her a patronizing look. "That's true, Jane, it's not boring."

"You almost got them to give chase to the scum that killed him," she said, motioning to the coffin. "I was there."

"Almost did, I suppose," said Fergus.

"Why didn't you boys follow that Plummer feller?" Jane asked. "He seemed to know what he was doing."

"I suppose we should have," said Fergus. "You two can go now. Just stay away from town."

Andrew was eager to go. "Come on," he said. "I want to show you something." He grabbed a tin bowl, a table knife, and a horsehair brush and led Jane down the path to a spot on the creek. Shadows lengthened in the late afternoon sun as miners dismantled their sluices. "The miners do a big cleanup of their sluices every Saturday," he said. "But they always leave some gold behind."

"You sure this is such a good idea?" asked Jane.

"Why?"

"Well, you're planning to take gold from these sluices, looks to me," she said.

"Yes."

"Well, there's a reason all these boys carry a gun on them while they's diggin' in the gravel."

"That's for claim jumpers," said Andrew. "They don't care about us."

Andrew set to work on one of the dismantled sluices. He used his knife blade and horsehair brush to extract bits of wet sand that sparkled with gold flake from the riffles: little cross-pieces nailed into the bottom of the sluice. Jane looked around to see who might take notice. To her surprise, a few miners leaned on shovels and watched them with tender smiles.

"How come they don't chase us off?" she asked. "It ain't like we are doing them a favor, taking their gold."

"They think it's cute," he said, "us being kids and all. None of these miners have families here. I bet I could get them to pay me to do this if I tried."

Andrew took the material he had pried out and brushed from the riffles, and placed it in the tin bowl.

"How do you get all the sand out?" Jane asked.

"Pan the sand out here in the creek, like this." He carefully swirled water and sand out of the bowl at the creek edge. "Then I heat it on the stove at home to get the black stuff out by blowing on it," he said.

Jane was intrigued by Andrew's new venture, but her mind snapped back to yesterday's events. "The coffin is for the Mormon, huh?" she said.

"Yeah."

"I saw him brung in," said Jane.

"My Dad says the trails ain't safe no how," said Andrew. "He says the trails are full of dead men."

The urge to confide in someone boiled inside Jane.

"My Dad says he doesn't know how we can get our money out of town," Andrew continued as he placed another dab of speckled sand in the bowl and dipped it in the creek. "He says... "

"Andrew, can you keep a secret?" Jane whispered.

Andrew paused his panning. "Sure," he said.

"You gotta promise, you can't tell no one."

"I promise," said Andrew.

"Not ever."

"Not ever. I ain't no blabbermouth," he said.

"I helped patch up the bandit what shot the Mormon," she whispered.

"The bandit!" Andrew said loudly as he rose from his crouch.

"Shh, shh," Jane hissed, as she looked around at the miners. Now she had done it. "You promised!" she said.

Andrew returned to the sluice he had been working. "Sure, sure. I can keep a secret."

Cat was out of the bag now, might as well tell the whole story. She described how Weasel-Snout and Glass-Eye brought Lefty, the injured bandit, to Glick, and described with pride how Glick made her his nurse. Of course, the arm had to be described in all its gory detail, and how Glick couldn't find the bullet no matter what, with the injured man swigging whiskey all along. She ended her tale saying, "and the reason you can't tell nobody is they said they would kill us if we told."

When Jane finally stopped, Andrew let out a whistle that began high-pitched and ended with a long, low tone.

"You can't tell no one," Jane said.

"I said I ain't no blabbermouth," Andrew replied. He scraped riffles silently. There was a long pause in the conversation.

"Who are these guys?" asked Andrew.

"Bandits," said Jane, shrugging.

"I mean, around town—who are these guys? You ever see them before?"

"No, of course not. These guys don't live in town. They prob'ly got a hideout somewhere."

"They probably do have a hideout. But I bet they come to town sometimes, for food and stuff," Andrew said.

"S'pose you're right," said Jane.

"There's a little poem I heard about this," said Andrew. "Goes like this:

> "So tell me, what was your name in the States?
> Was it Johnson or Thompson or Bates?
> Did you murder your wife?
> Did you flee for your life?
> So tell me, what was your name in the States?"

"I heard that one," Jane said. "So you think any tough guy you pass around here could be a bandit, huh?"

"Not these miners," Andrew said. "Look how they work. But my Dad says the bandits have lots of friends in the saloons, friends that were watching him yesterday."

"Anyhow, you'll keep the secret?"

"Sure, I told you." Andrew changed the subject. "There's a lady come to town last week, and word is, she's going to start a school."

"School is for soft folk back in the States," said Jane. "Ain't no use out here."

"What if your parents make you go?" asked Andrew.

"My folks ain't going to pay their food money for school to teach me stuff I don't need to know."

"I hate school," said Andrew.

"I can write my name, and read figures," said Jane. "That's all a body needs out here."

"My Mom says I hafta get a good education so's I can live in the States. I don't want to live in the States. I want to stay here."

"Me, too," Jane said. "What do you want to do when you grow up?"

"I want to be a rancher, raise cattle and stuff."

"You would make a good rancher." Jane nodded approvingly.

"What do you want to be when you grow up?" Andrew asked.

"I want to be a scout. I want to lead wagon trains all over the West, and hunt buffalo and antelope and all sorts of game."

"But you're a girl. How are you going to be a scout?"

"I can be a scout," said an indignant Jane. "Best ever, that's what the scouts that rode with us here from Missouri said. You seen me shoot."

"Sure, but what about the trains? My Dad says, soon as the war is over they're going to lay train tracks out here. Then people won't need scouts, they'll come by train."

Jane thought about that for a minute. "Then I'll hafta be an Indian fighter. Trains are bound to be attacked by Indians."

Andrew couldn't counter that reasoning. "If I hafta go to school, I won't have much time for hunting rabbits and panning for gold or any other fun stuff," he said.

"That would be a shame," she said. She felt sorry for her friend, but also wondered how she would fill her time if he went to school.

Chapter 6

The families of Bannack who had children and a little bit of money wasted no time finding a cabin for the new school now that they had a schoolteacher, and soon Dez, Andrew and the Kirkpatrick boys, James and Robert, were spending their days scratching out lessons on a handheld chalkboard.

Jane found herself at loose ends with her friends so occupied. Ma was still on her best behavior, so she did not have to watch Lana during the day as she had had to in the weeks leading up to their overnight stay with the Ferguses. Pa's fortunes still varied as much as before. Some days he would come home with a load of beans and flour and bacon from the store, and then some days they went hungry. Jane supplemented their meals with game, and Ma's laundry money helped, but most of the time there wasn't quite enough to go around.

One day Ma stretched a particularly sparse breakfast before the Canary family. "My money won't last to Saturday," she said.

"The easy gold for them miners is gone," said Pa. "There's tell that last year when they found gold in the creek, men just had to pull up clumps of grass and pan them for the flake in the roots. For a lark one day the boys washed the mud off'n the boots of a miner and got five dollars' worth of flake. Now, these boys dig all day and are damned lucky to get that much. Same as that, the take at a poker table ain't much neither."

"Winter could be hard around here," said Ma.

"Bound to be," said Pa. He scraped his plate clean with a piece of bread. "You hear of somewhere better, you let me know."

"Can't we go back home?" asked Lana.

Jane saw the accusatory looks Ma and Pa gave each other.

"This is home now, baby," was all Ma said.

After breakfast, Jane checked that her trusty rifle stood safely propped in the corner, but she went out the door without it. On her way to the bridge, she stopped to take in the activity of the swarming men who worked their diggings. They seemed to have an air of desperation now that she knew of the dwindling odds they faced, and she noticed for the first time how much deeper they dug now than when the Canarys had first arrived. Jane stood at the bridge and looked uphill towards town. Robert, Dez and James were on their way to a little cabin that served as their school. Robert scowled at her and turned away. Jane waved to Dez, but didn't seem to catch her eye.

Jane bounded over the bridge and headed up Main Street. Skinner's soon loomed ahead. Rumor was that an Indian chief's scalp was nailed prominently above the bar inside, taken from its owner by some coward who had murdered the peaceable old man. Anyhow, Jane had no inclination to see it for herself. She watched out of the corner of her eye for trouble as she passed that disreputable place. Her destination lay just ahead: Madam Chi's. The sign outside with a slinking, snarling Bengal tiger painted on it, enticed her to enter. Jane took a deep breath and stepped across the threshold of her destination. She waited for her eyes to adjust to the dark and acrid atmosphere. There was no fiddler to announce her presence today, and Jane thought she was unnoticed. Looking around, she was relieved to see that Greaseball was absent. She found Madam Chi dealing cards at a table full of men and approached.

"No more fireworks, Missy Calamity," said Chi. "You scare Southern boys with your 'bang-bang' too much. They not happy." The men around the table laughed heartily.

"I want to learn to deal cards," Jane told Chi. "For pay."

"Ah!" exclaimed Chi, a smile fleeting across her face. "You want take money from poor Madam Chi."

"I can bring in my own business. You start a new table, teach me the game. I will make you more money."

"How you know this?" asked Chi.

"Ask any of these boys," said Jane. "They would come here to play cards with a girl, I know it."

"She's probably right," said one of the men at the table.

"You smart girl," said Chi. "Lo!" she called out. Lo glided through the bead curtain that separated the gambling area from the back room. "Lo," Chi said, gesturing towards Jane. "You teach Faro."

Lo bowed, gave Jane a knowing smile, and led her to the back room. Jane's eyes were drawn to the shelf where Lo had previously pulled out the firecrackers, and her mind lit up with anticipation of what other oddments might be hidden in this room. Lo answered her unspoken question by pulling out a cloth-clad table-top with painted-on cards, an attached silver box, and embedded wires with beads on them. He dusted off this contrivance and placed it on a barrel head. "Losers sometime so angry," he said as his finger explored the soft green felt cloth, pointing out bullet holes to Jane, and watching for her reaction.

"That's the thing," said Jane. "They ain't gonna shoot up your place if a fifteen-year old girl is dealing, see?"

"Maybe you right," Lo said. He sat Jane down and pointed with long, steady fingers to the cards painted on the table, and showed how to keep track of what cards had been played on the wire and bead device, called a casekeep. He showed how players bet by placing their chips on cards they hoped would win and how a reverse bet was told by placing a certain marker on the bet.

Lo pulled a deck of cards from under his silk shirt and in doing so revealed the tattoo Jane had seen when she bought fireworks. He smiled when he saw that her gaze was drawn to his body adornment again. "This how game played," he said. He placed the deck of cards in the silver box and pulled four cards from the box one by one, placing them face up on the table. The first and last card were discards, he explained, and the second card won for the dealer those chips the players had placed on the corresponding painted-on cards (suits being ignored; only the value of the card mattered). The third card would win for the gambler, and the dealer had to pay from his or her own bank of chips. In the case of both the dealer's and the player's cards being the same number, the dealer won. After each round, the casekeep was reconciled, so that for the last round, everyone in the game knew which four cards remained. For this round of play, only the first card was discarded, and in order to win, players had to guess the order of the last three cards: a one-in-six possibility, which paid four to one.

"My Pa plays poker," Jane said. "Why don't you deal that here?"

Lo squinted. "Faro a game of chance. No bluffing, no skill like poker. Player drink hard at Faro table, no need keep track of cards... casekeep knows. Game for drinkers, not gamblers."

Jane's instruction took most of an hour, which included enough time to learn to shuffle the cards, with their Bengal tiger motif on the back. Finally, Lo sat back in his chair and gave Jane an enigmatic little smile, then pulled up his sleeve. "Jane remember this?" he said, showing her the tattoo on his arm.

"You promised to tell me the story," she said.

"Yes, yes, I promise tell you story! Now good time." He gathered up his thoughts. "See how I not teach you how dealer cheat? Yes? All other Faro table in town, in whole West they cheat. Not Lo. I not teach you. Lo honorable man." Then he leaned forward. "You know Masons?" he asked her.

Jane shook her head.

Lo continued, "Masons secret society. Only honorable men in Masons. First gold camp Lo start business, bad men rule. Robbery, murder every day, make Bannack look safe. Lo friends with good man, store owner name Hildebrandt. His English hard to understand, he speak German, but Hildebrandt good to Lo. One night, Hildebrandt sleep, three bad men shoot up store, kill Hildebrandt. Bad men take long time, search for money, not find. Lo and other men come see what happen, see Hildebrandt dead, see killers look for gold. Next day, good men meet. Good men want to chase killers, bring back to trial. Other men say, 'Killers have many friends, they killers, too.' Men say, 'No one brave enough testify against killers in trial.' " Lo looked at Jane. "You know 'testify?' " he asked.

Jane nodded. Of course she knew. But Lo, a grown-up from far-off China, did not know which words a fifteen-year-old American girl would know.

Lo continued. "Lo think, no can ride horse fast to catch killers, but Hildebrandt good friend to Lo. So Lo say 'Lo testify at trial. Lo testify against killers.' " Here Lo paused from his story and disappointment crossed his features. "Men say, different men say, 'no one believe Chinaman.' " Lo paused again. "Men laugh. Nobody do nothing. No one chase killers." Lo took a moment to regain his dignity. "Few men, days later say to Lo. 'You brave,' they say, 'You join Masons.' Men make Lo Mason."

"You're an honorary Mason?"

"Honorary!" Lo nearly spat in indignation. "Lo a Mason! You listen. Risk my life when say, 'Lo testify!' " He calmed down a bit. "You think like preacher. 'Heathen Chinee' say preacher." Lo pulled up his sleeve and held his arm close for Jane to examine the tattoo of the eye.

"Masons think, all men same under all-seeing eye of God. Lo a Mason."

"Got it. Lo a Mason," Jane said. "So, because you are honest, you don't make much money at Faro."

"Ah, Faro no make money." Lo waved his hand like swatting at a pesky fly. "Whiskey make money. You good girl. Fast learner. You come back tomorrow, Lo teach more."

The next day Jane hurried across the two-log bridge to Main Street and jogged uphill toward Madam Chi's. She gave Skinner's a wide berth again, wondering as she did where it was that Pa gambled. He never really said. She was past Skinner's when a shot rang out from its interior. The noise was so close that she turned reflexively toward the saloon. Nothing unusual now. Jane swung around again, eager to get to Chi's, and ran straight into a man carrying a sack.

"Watch where you're going," he growled. Then he recognized her, and she him. It was Weasel-Snout. "Ain't this something," he said. "Miss Jane, who won't let me call her Calamity." In an exaggerated movement, he doffed his hat and bowed to her. So Andrew had been right, she thought, the bandits do mingle among us. Jane was startled speechless, so she said nothing and proceeded on her way. "Hey, where's your manners, young-un?" he called after her, as she ducked into Madam Chi's.

The proprietress looked up from the crowded table she was working as Jane entered. She gave the deal to a man who had been watching and approached Calamity. Chi gave Jane an intent look. "Jane ready deal Faro?" she asked.

"I'm here to learn, Madam Chi," she said. "Where is Lo?"

"Lo busy now," said Chi. "Missy Calamity ready deal Faro?" she said, motioning to an empty table.

The run-in with Weasel-Snout evaporated from Jane's mind, replaced by excitement and anticipation. She thought of the first time she had entered this saloon and how exotic it had seemed. Then she reined in her excitement, thinking of Lana and her family's circumstances. "How much you pay?" she asked, instinctively mimicking Chi's speech pattern.

Madam Chi bowed. "Dollar an hour," she said.

Jane kept herself from jumping at the offer. She screwed up her face as she tried to figure out a counteroffer. She knew the price range for horses from swayback nag to champion racer. But she did not know the going rate for a Faro dealer in Bannack. "Two dollars an hour," she said.

"No! No!" said Chi. "Too much, too much. You no experience. No job here for two dollars." She folded her arms and looked insulted.

Jane was afraid now that Chi would withdraw the offer altogether. She really would have done it for free except that her family needed the money. "Okay, okay," she said, ready to cave. And then she saw the insulted look vanish from Chi's face for a moment—the Chinese woman was just bargaining. "Dollar fifty," Jane countered.

"No, no. Dollar twenty five."

So they settled at that price, and Chi led Jane to the empty Faro table, placed chairs for both herself and Jane at the table, and started shuffling a deck of cards. Men crowded around: this was something new, and the boys were always up for something new. At first Chi gave Jane the job of casekeeper, so she flicked beads on the wire device as cards were dealt, but when the men saw that Jane knew the game, they clamored for her to deal. Though Chi initially pretended to resist, she finally gave the card deck to Jane, who called out for bets as though she had been doing this her whole life. The men laughed heartily, and Jane felt as though she was among friends.

So started Jane's career as a Faro dealer. She dealt fast and efficiently day after day, and the smell of smoldering incense sticks came to identify Chi's place as her second home. When Lo watched from the shadows, he could see that Jane was a good student of the technique of the game. Chi taught Jane the art of being a good dealer: the banter that entertained men. She taught Jane to tease the men that liked teasing, and prod the men who were prideful. She taught her to be a bit more ladylike than was her natural tendency, toning down the cursing, getting her to hold her temper and letting little insults from the men slide off her. What the men came for when they sat down at Jane's table, Chi said, was the chance to banter with a member of the opposite sex. And what they wanted most was to banter with a refined woman, a good girl. So Jane became adept at banter—though maybe she still snuck in a swear word here and there—and her table became the most popular one around.

At the end of every day, Chi or Lo would pull out the gold scale and place a weight on one side and a folded paper on the other, and carefully weigh out Jane's wages in gold flake. Jane would then take the paper, pour it into a leather pouch, and swagger over to the dry goods store to buy whatever Ma needed that day.

One day, as Jane was dealing cards at her table and Madam Chi at hers, Greaseball entered and took a spot at Chi's table, Jane realized that she had never seen him except on his butt, as he had a noticeable limp. Greaseball flashed a malignant smile in Jane's direction. Soon followed a disreputable figure, who looked around for a moment, unfamiliar with the place. It was Weasel-Snout, who bought some chips from Lo and made his way to Jane's table, with Glass-Eye in tow. Weasel-Snout puffed himself up, and placed a reverse bet on a card.

"The new player wants to appear devious," Jane said as she pulled a card from the box.

"Just like to spice it up," said Weasel-Snout with a phony joviality.

Jane caught Greaseball and Weasel-Snout exchanging knowing glances. She did not break her stride, dealing and collecting chips, moving the marker on the casekeep wires between each deal.

"How comes it that one of our town's leading citizens graces us with his presence today?" said one of the other men at Jane's table.

"It's the novelty of it, boys," said Weasel-Snout. "I hear everyone in town wants to play Faro with the girl with spunk. And the price of her company is just a few poker chips." He surveyed the table. Then, cocking his head to one side, he placed bets on several cards. "Though I prefer games of skill to games of chance," he said.

"This ain't the only game in town," Jane countered.

The boys around the table chuckled, and that reaction gave Jane more confidence. She slid the next cards from the box and flipped them onto the table.

"Seems you are growin' up fast, Calamity," said Weasel-Snout.

"Told ya, name's Jane. My *friends* call me Calamity."

"You seem to have lots of friends," said Weasel-Snout. "How come I can't be one of them?"

"Think a little harder. You might be able to figure that one out." Jane could feel her own movements becoming more guarded. She wasn't sure what Weasel-Snout was up to, but she wanted to show that she wasn't going to be intimidated. All the while, she flipped cards, moving beads on the casekeep after each round, taking chips when she won, paying winning bettors out of her bank. But her pace slowed, and her smile disappeared.

Weasel-Snout collected on a bet. "Your Ma know you're here?"

"Sure does," Jane replied.

"We all know she's a special lady, your Ma," said Weasel-Snout. "I suppose you want to grow up to be just like her."

The silence was broken by a snicker from Greaseball.

"I could do worse," Jane said.

Weasel-Snout nodded. "Things can always get worse, my dear Jane." He placed chips on the jack. There was a cold smirk on his lips, and his eyes were like daggers.

Jane resumed her deal, and flipped up a five, then a jack. "Jack to the dealer." She raised her eyebrows, then adroitly scooped up his chips.

Weasel-Snout whistled and leaned back in his chair, allowing his coat to fall and reveal his revolver. Jane continued flipping cards.

"Well, seems Lady Luck don't shine on me today. Not here anyhow." Weasel-Snout pushed back from the table and, with the same malignant smile, rose to his feet.

"I just had to see the newest game in town for myself. Looks good. All business. First-rate Faro table...Jane. You shouldn't work here though. Not a fit place for a white girl."

"They treat me good here," said Jane.

"Problem is, these opium dens, they go up in flames all the time," said Weasel-Snout.

"This ain't no opium den," said Jane, "any more than you are the King of England."

"Just the same," said Weasel-Snout, "I wouldn't be surprised to find the place burned to the ground one day. Just sayin'," as he walked to the door.

"You walk funny," said Jane. "Like you ain't recovered since the last time we said good-bye."

Weasel-Snout glared at her wordlessly, jerked his head for Glass-Eye to follow him, and headed out the door into the midday light.

After they left, Jane felt a wave of relief. "All bets in," she said.

Chapter 7

There came to be a certain rhythm to Jane's days. It was not a tedium, a grind, or a rut, but her days had a certain predictability. She didn't work at Madam Chi's on a schedule, but after every stint at the Faro table she would tell Chi when to expect her next. She saw Andrew or Dez from a distance now and then, but rarely more than that. It was fun being the center of attention at the Faro table, but she missed the company of Andrew especially.

Visits to the dry goods store were part of Jane's routine. One fine summer day, not long after Weasel-Snout's visit, she headed there on the way home, intending to buy flour for Ma and hard candy for herself and Lana. Today, though, something was afoot. A crowd milled around the store, talking excitedly among themselves. There were so many people that it would have been impossible for her to get any attention inside, so Jane waited. Shortly, two scruffy-looking men emerged with sacks of goods and headed down the street, followed by the crowd. Even as she watched, the crowd grew in numbers and excitement, with men running to join in. Jane was very curious herself. She followed the crowd for a bit, but didn't see anyone she knew, and all were too caught up in the excitement to pay her any attention. So she ambled into the store. Over the past few weeks Jane had become familiar with the proprietor, a Mr. Ben Ezekial. He always treated her nicely. Bannack was full of men who missed their families back in the States.

A customer was finishing a purchase and said to Mr. Ezekial, "I seen this all before. Felt like a fool last stampede I went on—turned out to be a total bust." He left Jane and the storekeeper in an otherwise empty store.

"Calamity, my darling," Mr. Ezekial called out, more cheerily than usual. Here was another sort Jane would have never met in Missouri, this kindly Jewish man from New York City.

"What's all the commotion?" Jane asked.

"Looks like a stampede is on."

"I seen a buffalo stampede before, but I never seen the two-legged kind," said Jane.

"It's part of the very fabric of life in a mining district," said Mr. Ezekial. "The gold here is nearly played out, right? Pretty soon they will be scraping bedrock in the creek."

"I heard that," Jane said.

"So there's boys prospecting up in the hills all the time. Now, any time some boys come back from prospecting, makes sense to watch them, if you are a miner anyway. Wouldn't you agree?"

"S'pose."

"Sure," he continued. "These boys, if they made a big find, they're going to try to hide it. They want all the gold for themselves. They try to be coy. But everyone watches them. Rumors start."

"What about what this last guy said?" Jane motioned out the door. "How do you know it's for real?"

"Here, my dear Calamity," he said, and he pulled a gold sack from under the counter. "See this? This is the gold dust that comes out of Bannack Creek."

The gold was in tiny flakes, with specks of black scattered in it, just like she had first seen in Andrew's inkwell and been paid with a couple dozen times since. "I seen that before," she said. As far as she knew, that was what all gold looked like.

"Now look here," Mr. Ezekial said. He showed her a folded paper full of lustrous gold nuggets. Most were the size of pinheads, but some were larger. "This is how they paid me just now. This doesn't come from around here. So while these boys try to sneak around town and keep their mouths shut, their gold speaks loud and clear."

Jane felt Mr. Ezekial's excitement, and it was infectious. Visions of bags of gold danced in her head.

An excited-looking man burst in. He ran up to Ezekial. "I need rope," he said.

"Dollar-fifty a pound," said Ezekial.

"But the sign says a dollar a pound," the man protested.

"This morning that was just rope," said Ezekial. "Now it is pack animal cinch rope, and you are a wise man to be buying it at this time, while I still have some left." He winked at Jane.

The man decided that Ezekial had a point, so he bought his rope, and Jane bought the flour and candy she had come for. She thanked Mr. Ezekial, then caught up with the crowd that was following the prospectors, for a time bathing in its excitement. The crowd was single-minded in its fervor, but quiet for such a large gathering. The men were listening for clues and playing along with the prospectors, who were still trying to be nonchalant, saying nothing much and giving each other sidelong glances.

Jane spotted her acquaintance Cecil in the crowd. The gentle giant saw her as well and gave her a big smile, his white teeth fairly blazing against the rest of his dark face. Jane squeezed her way through the crowd to his side.

"I hear there's a stampede on," she said.

"Looks like you are right, Missy, yes you are," he replied.

"Who are these boys?" said Jane, indicating the prospectors who were leading the crowd around by its figurative nose.

"These boys are Fairweather and Edgar."

"You think they found something?"

"They bought near half Mr. Ezekial's store, so stands to reason," he said.

"You goin' on the stampede?" Jane asked.

"Be a fool not to, Missy," he said with another big smile.

"What if there ain't enough for everybody?" asked Jane.

"Could happen that way, but this is my chance to stake my own claim. Besides, the town's going to be near empty when this stampede leaves. Won't be no one left to pay me wages."

Jane took a moment to picture an empty Bannack, thanked Cecil, and squeezed her way back out of the crowd. She ran towards home, holding her groceries tightly as she scampered downhill to the creek, then practically hopped over the log bridge. She arrived at her cabin all out of breath, though whether more from exertion or excitement there was no telling.

Jane knew something was amiss as soon as she burst through the canvas flaps. The cabin had a foul smell of blood and vomit. Before her eyes could adjust to the dark, Ma led her back outside. "Pa's sick," she said.

"How sick?" Jane patted Queenie, who whined and wagged her tail timidly as she did when she thought she had done something wrong.

"Sick," said Ma. "But Doctor Glick says he might be okay if he stops drinking." Lana clung to Ma's skirt.

Dr. Glick emerged from the cabin. "For now, it seems the bleeding has stopped. Give him some baking soda, and If there's no more bleeding overnight, he's probably out of danger." He picked up his leather bag and tipped his hat to Ma. "You know where to reach me."

"There's a stampede on," said Jane.

Glick stopped and cocked his head towards her, one eyebrow raised and his lips pursed. "Don't say. Well, y'all can follow later, if it turns out to be anything."

Jane approached Glick as he secured his bag on the saddle of his regal white horse. "One of them boys paid me a visit over at Madam Chi's," she said.

"I heard you have been making a quite a name for yourself dealing Faro," he said. "I'm sorry I got y'all involved in this."

"That don't make no never mind, Doc," said Jane. "But they threatened to burn down Chi's place."

"I wish I could make it right," he said.

"Some guy at my Faro table called that boy 'a leading citizen.' What the hell did he mean by that?"

" 'Leading citizen' is a flowery term for the riff-raff that is always being banished from one frontier town to the next, on the furthest edge of the West."

"So everybody knows he's a bandit?" Jane asked.

"Unsavory character, anyhow. Lucky is doing fine, by the way," said Glick, as he swung his leg up on his mount. He tipped his hat to Jane and spurred his horse homeward.

Pa did have a quiet night. The next morning while he and Lana slept, Jane helped Ma make breakfast. Ma looked awfully worried. She looked at the pot she stirred and said quietly to Jane, "Don't reckon what you and I make would keep us in beans and biscuits."

"I should go on the stampede," Jane said.

"Most certainly not, little lady!" Ma said.

"Ma, you should see the gold these boys brought in. There's a ton of it. Giant nuggets and stuff."

"You have really gone off your rails," said Ma. "You are barely fifteen, if I have to remind you of that. You think you could just follow a stampede by yourself?"

"I bet the Ferguses would take me," said Jane.

"Darlin'," said Ma. "The Ferguses think your Pa and me are vermin—or, truth is, lower than vermin for leavin' you and Lana on your own that night. I ain't givin' them the satisfaction of thinkin' I ain't learned to keep an eye on you."

"Ma," said Jane. "Ain't going to be hardly no one left in town when the stampede leaves. You can't make no money on laundry if there ain't no miners' clothes to wash. I can't make no money at Faro. And now Pa is sick." She looked Ma in the eye. "I got to go."

Ma looked at the ground. "You prob'ly think the same as the Ferguses and their kind anyhow. Well, if you can find someone to take you, go. S'pose the least I can do now is get the hell out of your way."

"Thanks, Ma," Jane said. Ma leaned forward for a hug, but Jane wasn't ready for that yet. After she finished her breakfast, Jane headed towards town.

Bannack sang a different song this morning. Normally there would have been the rough sound of gravel being shoveled from stream to sluice and back out again by dozens of men, but now the sounds of breaking camp met Jane's ears. The cursing of the miners was at the same intensity as always, but the men's focus was on sorting through gear and packing up what could be carried. The street was busy with men hurrying back and forth from their cabins to the store or the blacksmith, the saloons quiet. Jane crossed the bridge and headed up Main Street. Ma was right: the Ferguses were not her best bet on this venture. Jane pushed open the door of her employer. Madam Chi's was empty, the Faro tables strangely idle, save for Lo and Chi sitting at one table, engaged in an animated discussion.

"Morning, Madam Chi, Lo," said Jane.

"Calamity," Chi said.

"You goin' on the stampede?" Jane asked.

"Stampede not for Chinaman. Chi and Lo wait," Chi said. "If good diggings, we follow, make new saloon."

Lo seemed less certain that this was the best course.

"Looks like no money to be made in Bannack, anyhow," Jane said.

"Stampede for round-eyes, not Chinaman," said Lo, hesitantly. He paused and looked at Jane. "Jane not know, men take from Chinaman what men want. End up lose everything. Better go later."

"What if we went together? Same as they won't shoot up a Faro table here 'cause I'm a girl, I can be your protection on the stampede 'cause I'm a white girl."

Lo's eyes narrowed. He looked at Chi, who folded her arms.

"Much to carry. Need horses. Lo never buy horses," said Chi. "Not know good horse from buffalo dung."

Jane saw Lo flinch. Probably true, but it was a harsh assessment. Lo and Chi must have been in a heated argument about this issue.

Falling into her employers' speech pattern unintentionally, she said, "Jane knows horses. Find Lo good horses."

Jane had learned to read these two over time, but she couldn't read them now. "You smart girl, smart girl," Lo said finally. He turned to Madam Chi and the two exchanged sharp words back and forth in their own tongue until Madam Chi seemed to give in. Lo turned to Jane and said, "Lo and Jane go on stampede. No business here. Jane know horses."

Jane jumped up, bursting with excitement. "Let's get a move on, then!"

So Jane and Lo went about town, hunting up what they needed for their adventure. Lo bought a few items from Mr. Ezekial, including the last few yards of rope at the exorbitant price of $3.50 a pound, and he was glad to pay it, for how else could they strap kegs of whiskey to their pack animals? Finding horses proved more difficult than Jane had anticipated, and they came up empty-handed on the first pass through town. But they eventually found men who Jane convinced to part with a couple mules- one that could carry supplies, and another beauty named Black Bess that would be Lo's steed. Lo paid triple what he would have paid a week before, but there was no alternative. Jane finally found a spirited Indian cayuse pony for herself; it was too small for most men, but just the right size for her. Once these transactions had been completed, Jane felt absolutely exhilarated. Now she was to return to her natural element—the great outdoors, on horseback. A vision danced through her mind of the Canarys living in a log cabin in the new town, just like the one in which the Ferguses lived now, with a sewing machine that Ma would use to make Lana nice dresses, and a neat little towel sewn into a loop over a towel rod for all the Canarys to use to wash up. This time, her family was going to be among the early arrivals to the new diggings.

Chapter 8

The morning of the rumored stampede arrived. Rumored, that is, because although it was obvious that nearly the entire town was pulling up stakes to follow them, Fairweather and Edgar were still playing coy. A crowd of two hundred or more milled about the pair of prospectors as they made what appeared to be their final preparations. Some in the crowd were afoot, loaded with just what gear they thought essential, while others were outfitted like Lo and Jane with horses and pack animals. Excitement charged the air around the churning assemblage, and the noise from men and animals alike was deafening. Among this mass of humanity, diverse as it was, one would have been hard-pressed to find a more incongruous pair than the Chinaman in pigtails, sitting heavily astride his sturdy mule, and the brash girl in boys' clothes who rode so naturally on her nimble cayuse pony, squirrel gun holstered within easy reach. Either alone was a sight, but as a pair they looked positively comical.

Jane spied Andrew and the Kirkpatrick boys at the edge of the dust cloud churned up by the crowd. Andrew waved; the other two just looked sullen. Guess not everyone is making tracks today, Jane thought. She took leave of Lo to saunter over to the boys on horseback. Brothers James and Robert looked progressively more awkward as Jane approached.

"Howdy," she said to all. She hadn't seen much of these boys since school had started.

"Where'd ya get that horse?" said Robert.

Jane patted the neck of her steed. "This here is one fine Indian pony, straight up. I call him Lightning."

"Looks like a midget horse that somebody spilled paint on," said Robert.

"You wanna race him with that swayback nag that pulls your wagon?" Jane shot back.

"Bet it don't make it over the next ridge, loaded like that on them stubby little legs," Robert said.

Jane felt her temper rising, her jaw set for a fight, her muscles tensing. Andrew gave her a look, and she decided instead to draw on a new skill instead. She shrugged and nodded almost imperceptibly, paused for effect, then looked at her foe. "How's school goin', Robert?"

Her bullet hit its mark. A dejected silence fell over Robert. As Jane had suspected, he was jealous, aching to go on the stampede.

"Andrew!"

"Aw, it's my Mom," Andrew said.

"Seems to have a bee in her bonnet," said Jane.

"She don't like it when girls ride like that."

Jane swiveled around to inspect her steed. "Ride like what?" she said.

"You know," he said, pointing at her leg.

"Can't say I do," said Jane. She looked at the brothers, who couldn't bring themselves to look at her.

Then it occurred to her. "Oh, astride," she said. Polite womenfolk, those who didn't swear and didn't drink, also would only ride sidesaddle. And they didn't use the word "astride" in mixed company. Andrew blushed.

"Come on," Jane said. "You three are acting like I'm tryin' to describe my undies to you."

"Andrew, you come here now," said Mrs. Fergus.

"Just a minute, Mom!" Andrew called. "I gotta go," he said to Jane. "My Dad says if this stampede is the real thing he'll send for us."

"Oh, it's the real thing," said a cocky Jane. "So that means I'll see you soon." With that, she wheeled Lightning around on his stubby little legs and rode back to Lo.

There was no starting gun fired, no shouted announcement to start the stampede. The two prospectors, Fairweather and Edgar, started at their own pace, still studiously ignoring the throng that surrounded them. The men of the stampede, plus Jane and a few dance hall girls, followed the prospectors downstream along the creek in a chaotic parade. Strewn a quarter-mile or more behind their reluctant leaders, they excitedly crushed a swath of sage fifty yards wide as they went. The dust was so thick that it coated throats and caused eyes to tear. Jane had expected dust like this. "Wish I had a nice red bandana," she muttered as she pulled a coarse cloth out of her pocket. Lo had never before had the experience of being able to eat the same air he breathed. As he told her, he had come to Bannack by narrow mountain trails from Canada. His present suffering was relieved when Jane ripped her cloth and gave him half.

Jane had never before seen anything as exciting as this stampede. It was as if every saloon in Bannack had decided on a whim to go on an expedition, with singing and shouting and good-natured cursing all about. The crush of sage underfoot sounded like a dozen simultaneous threshing-times back on the farm. Mules brayed, and men had to practically shout just to be heard by their partners. Every few hundred yards, someone's horse would step in a gopher hole and take a tumble, spilling the rider and usually strewing hastily-packed gear on the ground amid a torrent of cursing. Jane was proud of Lightning as he nimbly kept up with the rest. Lo, awkward as he was on his mule, maintained an admirable level of dignity.

Fairweather and Edgar led the stampede along the creek for the few miles of territory it traversed until it emptied into a river. Here, Jane had passed all the landmarks with which she was familiar. She pulled down her bandana for a moment. "Lo," she shouted above the din, "how far you reckon we have to travel?"

"Prospectors gone one month. Maybe you hear, Crow Indians attack, kill one. You ready for two week trip?" he asked.

Jane thought that somehow that didn't seem right. She rode up closer to Lo so he didn't have to shout.

"They not pack much food," Lo continued. "Not far. Few days most."

The journey settled into tedium. The crush of humanity that made up the stampede came to a muddier area that had been flooded in spring by a beaver dam. As a result, the dust abated, allowing a view of the surrounding wilderness. The lush greenery of the riverbed was surrounded by parched brown foothills. The parent mountains of those foothills loomed far in the distance. Jane searched for Fairweather and Edgar at the head of the throng and saw them engaged in conversation with Plummer, the former sheriff with the refined manners. The three engaged in earnest conversation for a while, with Plummer projecting an air of knowledgeability and confidence. They separated, and Fairweather and Edgar spoke between themselves as if considering what Plummer had advised.

Fairweather and Edgar led their eager, slow-motion cavalcade out of the muddy area, and a dust cloud again formed, obscuring the leaders from Jane's view. There was a brief stop for a cold meal, and then they pressed on. Jane was exuberant as she contemplated her future, and sang songs to entertain herself and Lo. Her past seemed of no consequence at this moment, and her future unlimited. They were led up a creek as the sun approached the horizon behind them to the west. The entire stampede slowed: they were going upstream and uphill.

Lo motioned Jane close to him. "If this is creek, we very close—creek too small—not go far up mountain."

Fairweather and Edgar stopped their horses and dismounted. Fairweather acknowledged the crowd for the first time. "We'll camp here," he said loudly, and the multitude followed suit.

That night, Jane slept under the stars on the grassiest spot she could find, with only her bedroll blanket for cover and her saddle for a pillow. As the camp noise faded, she examined the stars in the sky, and found the North Star out of habit. The heavens seemed to be a fitting symbol for the infinite possibilities which lay before her. But her thoughts soon returned to Earth. This was the first night she could remember in which she couldn't lull herself to sleep with her sister's rhythmic breathing. And how was Pa tonight? They

didn't get along much lately, but she still cared about him. In her mind, she imagined a new home for her family, with an actual door with leather hinges, curtains decorating a greased paper window and food in the pantry. With those images dancing before her eyes, she fell asleep.

The next morning, Fairweather and Edgar seemed in even less of a hurry. They made breakfast over a campfire and leisurely repacked their horses. Jane and Lo ate a cold breakfast so they could move on at a moment's notice. They didn't have to be first to the discovery, but they didn't want to be last either. Jane did her part to pack up and decided to take a walk around camp.

Men were aggregated in small groups of a half-dozen or more, joking and planning excitedly amongst themselves. Jane saw Cecil and waved to him. His group included a Mexican and another dark-skinned fellow. Cecil waved back and held up some wooden stakes for her to see. Jane sauntered over.

"Morning, Missy Calamity," he said.

"What you got there?" Jane asked.

"See? Carved my own name in these. Gonna stake my own claim, Missy, just like I told you before. Gonna work for myself this time."

"Who's this guy?" she said, referring to Cecil's dark-skinned companion, who, deep as that darkness was, did not look African. The muscular fellow regarded her with a toothy smile.

"That's one of my new partners. He's from the Solomon Islands. You ever heard of the Solomon Islands?"

"I heard of the Sandwich Islands," said Jane.

"Oh, well," said Cecil, "the Solomon Islands are much more exotic than that." He leaned forward in a conspiratorial manner. "There's cannibals on the Solomon Islands, you know. He doesn't speak much English. Seems to like you, though."

Right on cue, as if he had played this joke a hundred times before on the unsuspecting, the Solomon Islander licked his lips slowly. Jane withdrew reflexively, prompting gales of laughter from Cecil and his partners.

Jane recovered. "Don't you turn your back on him; you'd make him a lot more meals than me," she told Cecil, who roared with laughter again.

Jane continued to roam the camp. A group of Germans plotted their day in their own guttural language, and further along she heard the lovely lilt of an Irish clan doing the same. She spotted Mr. Fergus, who waved her over. "Good morning, Jane. How do you like the stampede so far?" Evidently he had lost his hat and picked up another one somewhere that was too small for his head, for he had cut slits in the band of It so that it would expand to fit. His hair stuck out of these slits in a manner that looked a bit ridiculous. Mr. Fergus seemed less aloof than previously to Jane, and maybe it was partly the hat.

"Suits me fine. You gonna become a miner?"

"I don't plan to shovel any gravel, but I can pound a stake in the ground," said Fergus. "Hard part is fending off claim jumpers."

"You armed?"

"My partners are," he said with a smile. "For better or worse, I'm more the brains of the outfit."

Plummer appeared out of the crowd and walked towards them with the measured gait of a man who knew where he was going, tipping his hat to Mr. Fergus as he passed. He continued toward Fairweather and Edgar, with whom he spoke earnestly. He then climbed up on a rock and fired his big Navy revolver in the air three times. Stampeders gathered around on that signal and Plummer gave Fairweather a hand up on the rock, then stepped down. Fairweather raised his arms for quiet.

"You boys think we found another Bannack here, don't you?" he shouted.

The crowd responded with cheers and shouts, and clamored for more.

"Well, you're wrong."

Moans and cursing followed.

Fairweather's eyes twinkled, for anyone that was close enough to see. "Bannack wasn't nothin' compared to this find, boys!"

The crowd roared its response. "Lead the way!" someone shouted.

Fairweather, still on the rock, held up his hands and called for quiet. "You had better believe me that we would rather let our horses die at the end of their tethers than to stir a foot in the direction of the discovery, lessen certain matters are settled. So first things first! I declare a miner's meeting in session."

Jane bid Mr. Fergus goodbye and made her way back to Lo. She had seen several miner's meetings before, but never one like this. The miner's meetings that were held every Sunday in Bannack usually dealt with mundane, boring issues such as infringement on water rights, and most who attended did so for lack of other entertainment after their money had run out. Compared to those miner's meetings, this one was a highly energetic and single-minded affair.

Fairweather proposed that he and Edgar be awarded two claims, which they had already staked, with the stipulation that they be inviolate from claim jumping. This seemed unfair to many, since their own claims would still be subject to that risk, and there were some tepid protests, but this was accepted. Rules were then adopted regarding claim length along the stream bed and how water had to be returned to the stream, and so forth. They allowed for miner's meetings every Sunday, and specified that matters put to a vote were to be settled by a simple majority. A claim had to be worked a certain number of days every week or it was forfeit, Fairweather and Edgar's claim again excepted. As Fairweather proposed his rules for the district one by one, it seemed to Jane that this group would approve anything set before them, if it meant that they would be pointed in the direction of the discovery a moment sooner. Finally, Fairweather held up his arms for quiet. The crowd was restless, and it took some time before things settled down. He was in no hurry; his claim was already staked.

"Miner's court adjourned," yelled Fairweather. "Now boys, it's time to git. See that grove of alder trees yonder? That's it. Just upstream of that..."

An explosion of noise drowned out whatever else he said. There was an immediate clatter of dropped items as men on foot rushed for the grove. Those on foot had a head start, but those on horseback quickly overtook them after cutting their loads loose as well. The stampede was undergoing its last spasm to the desired conclusion, and every man wanted to be the first to the new El Dorado.

Jane looked at Lo and saw his impassive face and relaxed demeanor, unaffected by the pandemonium, impervious to gold fever. She, however, found the disease more contagious. With Lo's permission, she galloped after the body of stampeders, skillfully weaving her Indian pony between the hastily dumped piles of paraphernalia. She passed the trotting miners on foot as they panted and called out to one another to hurry.

Past the alder grove, Jane reined in her pony to survey the scene of the stampede's chaotic terminus. It turned out that Edgar and Fairweather had had their friends sneak out the night prior so they could be there to protect their claims. These were the only men who were motionless: guarding their claims, rifles at the ready. All other new arrivals were engaged in frantic activity. The most valuable claims were assumed to be the ones closest to Fairweather and Edgar's, so some raced there. Others scattered up and downstream, picking the inside bend of the stream first, as that was usually the richest spot. Cecil and his partners headed far upstream and out of sight, seeking a stretch of the creek that they would not have to defend so vigorously from claim jumpers. For all anyone knew, that was where the richest claims were anyway.

As Jane watched, Lo sidled up to her on Black Bess, leading the other mule with its precious load of booze and gambling equipment. "Town over there," he said, pointing to high ground across the river. "Soon they thirsty."

Over the next few hours the incredible richness of the new find became apparent. The first hour of activity was frenetic claim staking; the next few hours saw some miners panning gold and finding nuggets in nearly every pan or shovelful, others cutting trees for shelter. Jane and Lo built a rough shelter out of brush and poles. By the afternoon they had set up the crudest of drinking establishments and their first customers were slaking their thirst and gambling the first nuggets they had found. That night their business got underway in earnest. Jane dealt Faro by kerosene lamp, intermittently brushing leaves off the table that fell from the rustic ceiling. A large number of men passed their first evening in the new Alder Camp crowded around Lo's pole-and-brush emporium. Lo sold his whiskey to carefree men who were already intoxicated with gold fever, and he made money hand over fist. As Jane pulled cards from the little silver box on the Faro table, the excitement of it all felt as though she was riding her beloved Lightning through a herd of buffalo.

Chapter 9

Lo woke Jane the next morning before the sun crested over the mountains to the east. "Lo make breakfast. Eat quick, we go."

"Go where?" asked Jane.

"Whiskey almost gone. Madam Chi have more back Bannack."

"What if someone jumps this place?" Jane asked.

"No one jump this place. Mr. Fergus stay here."

Jane was reluctant to miss a minute of the excitement of the new Alder Camp, as it was called now, but Pa's health tugged at her consciousness, and as always she worried about Lana as well. She ate her breakfast and scanned the camp. Men stirred from where they had slept, which for many was no more than a depression dug out under an overhang of rock. No wonder Mr. Fergus was willing to watch their place. Dozens of campfires filled the air with wisps of smoke, and dozens more were in the making, with men gathering wood and fetching water from the stream for coffee.

Jane heaved her saddle onto her pony. As she cinched it, she noticed Lo hide something in his boot. She walked over to him. "If that's money, I should take it," she said. Lo hesitated. "Same reason you got me along in the first place," said Jane.

Lo agreed, and Jane discreetly slung the sack down her pants leg and suspended it on its drawstring. She then put her squirrel gun in its holster on the front of her saddle. Though such a small caliber weapon was scant protection, it comforted her to see it there, the well-worn maple stock sticking up at a ready angle.

They mounted their steeds, with an unburdened mule trailing behind, and headed across Alder Creek. On the opposite bank, Jane could survey a long stretch of the muddy stream. As far as the eye could see, claims lined Alder, with men everywhere having breakfast over campfires or at work clearing brush, building shelters, or working the gravel for all it was worth. These latter men were at the stream's edge, using freshly built "rockers"—one-man devices that looked like baby cradles, with which they worked gold out of the gravel. She touched the gold sack at her thigh for reassurance and spurred her pony onwards.

Soon they came to the campsite where all the gear had been dumped on the ground for the last mad dash. Everything had been retrieved except scraps of food that some crows picked at, hopping and cawing as they jostled each other. The whole area had been trampled so much that Jane could not recognize where she had slept that night, trying so hard to imagine what lay before her. They proceeded downstream to where they came in sight of the river and there turned upstream towards Bannack. The breeze in the leaves of the cottonwood trees whispered a soothing song, accompanied by the babble of the river, music that had been drowned out during the stampede.

The trail back to Bannack was easy to follow. What an amazing difference a day could make on the frontier, Jane mused. Her thoughts turned to her family. Could Pa travel soon, or would they be late arrivals to the goldfields again and be forced to scrape out a meager existence?

The morning half of the trip was pleasant and uneventful. They had their lunch of biscuits and dried fruit at the stretch that had been flooded by the beaver dam, since here there was ample grass for their animals. Jane kept an eye on the trail in both directions, watching for trouble, so she was first to spot the dust trail of a dozen or so horsemen approaching from Bannack. "We might have company," she said.

Lo stood and squinted in the direction of the horsemen. "Just travelers," he said. "Too many for bandits."

Jane wasn't so sure. She fondled the maple stock of her squirrel gun. "You ever shoot a gun?" she asked Lo.

"No," he grunted.

The men that approached looked exhausted and desperate. Their leader reined in his horse. "Howdy, son."

"Name's Jane." Most in Bannack knew Jane well enough that they saw past the boys' attire she wore. Jane found the greeting kind of funny, but she didn't feel she could relax enough around this bunch to crack a smile yet.

"No offense meant, Miss."

"None taken," she replied.

"We heard there might be a new gold find in this direction."

"You wouldn't have to be Kit Carson to follow this trail." Jane indicated the trampled trail with a wave.

"Is it true?" interjected one of the other men.

"We ain't miners, but seems like the boys found some color," Jane said.

"All the claims staked, you think?" asked the second man.

"It's a pretty long creek," Jane replied. She felt more relaxed. The line of questioning pretty well indicated that these men wouldn't rob them. They were desperate, but just desperate to get to Alder before the last claim had been staked.

At any rate, what little Jane told them seemed to inspire the men to hurry onwards. They tipped their hats to Jane and, still ignoring Lo, and galloped in the direction of Alder.

Jane and Lo mounted and resumed their journey. Lo rode in front of Jane and forcefully called out invectives in Chinese as he bumped along. Finally he seemed to have gotten it all off his chest. He paused for a minute or so, then turned in his saddle and addressed her. "Lo, the invisible Chinaman. Ha!"

"Don't worry, Lo, I see you just fine," Jane said.

Lo shrugged, gave Jane a sly smile, and let out another loud "Ha!"

The sun cast long shadows that were a mute prelude to the coming sunset. The incongruous pair crossed the river at the mouth of the creek to Bannack. They were close to home, and Jane felt her tensed muscles relax. The mules slowed as the trail climbed a grade that curled toward a rocky promontory. Jane thought of how exciting it would be to tell Lana and Ma and Pa about the stampede and the new camp on Alder Creek. Their mounts slowed more as the grade steepened. Jane kept her eyes down to avoid the glare from the low-angled sun.

Suddenly, four horsemen burst from the cover of the rocky out-cropping. "Hands in the air or I'll blow the tops of your heads off!" one yelled. Jane reined in Lightning, startled, her heart pounding. She could see the gunmen silhouetted against the sun well enough to tell that they wore flour sacks for masks, and blankets covered their horses. Lo put up his hands immediately, but at first Jane did not comprehend that they intended the command for her as well.

"And you too, me Lassie," said another of the bandits. She raised her arms, and felt the leather pouch shift against her thigh.

One rider sidled up to her and pulled her gun from its holster.

"I'll take this," he said.

"Hey, give that back!" she said. "It's just a squirrel gun."

"You'll get it back. Just don't want you starting anything you can't finish."

"You know what we want, Chinee," the leader said to Lo.

"In my shirt. I reach for it, or you take it?" Lo asked.

Jane was impressed that he had not the slightest tremor in his voice. His example inspired calm in her as well.

"That's a good bhoy," said the leader. "We'll take it. Keep yer arms high." He motioned to one of the other men, who dismounted and patted Lo down.

"That's the most awful phony Irish accent I ever heard," said Jane, keeping her hands raised.

"Never ye mind me Lassie, ye kin wait your turn," said the leader. A small sack of gold was found on Lo, which was tossed to the leader. He weighed it in his palm. "Where's the rest?" he said.

"Lo not stupid. Rest buried back there," he jerked his head in the direction of Alder.

"We'll see," the leader said.

He directed the other men to dismount and unpack all of Jane and Lo's effects while he covered them with his rifle. One of them limped as he scrambled around. When the "bhoys" came up empty-handed, the leader turned to Jane.

"Hand me yours," he said.

"How do you know I've got any, stranger?" asked Jane.

"No foolin' around, Lassie. Hand me your buckskin."

"You wouldn't rob a poor little girl like me, would you?" she said.

"Don't keep us waiting any longer," the bandit with the limp blurted, "or I'll cut your ears off!" Yep, thought Jane, even as he drew his Bowie knife, that's him. That's Greaseball.

"I ain't paid much," said Jane. "Is yer heart all gizzard?"

"Pull it out now!" said Greaseball. "I ain't foolin'."

Jane could see by the fact that he had dropped the phony accent that he was nervous, more nervous than she was. "Sure, stranger," she drawled. "Then take it." She tossed him a buckskin pouch, but not the fat one Lo had given her; it was her own, which had just about a couple days' pay in it. "And if you think I got any more, search me!" She made a defiant twisting motion with her upraised arms.

"Put yer hands down and dismount," said the leader.

Jane complied, with an unconcerned attitude. "Search me then. But do it here. I don't want you getting your jollies at my expense behind some bush."

"Get to it, then," said the leader to Greaseball.

"I ain't no pervert," he said. "You search her."

"Ah, she ain't got nothing," said one of the others. "Come on, boys, let's go."

"We ain't got hardly nothin' for our trouble," said Greaseball.

"What do you suggest we do then?" said the leader.

"I ain't saying nothin'. Just, you know who ain't going to like it."

"You two are gettin' off easy this time," said the leader. "Next time you take this trail, you better have more money, or it will be much worse for you. Come on, boys." He spurred his horse and galloped away from the trail, and the others followed.

Jane and Lo watched the bandits long enough to see that they were indeed gone. Then they turned to repacking the items the "bhoys" had strewn about, no doubt as part of a ploy to delay them. Jane picked up her rifle first and sighted down the barrel.

"Leastwise you weren't invisible that time," she said.

Lo looked Jane in the eye. "What you mean, I don't pay you much?" he said playfully. They shared a laugh.

"I think we both know one of those boys," said Jane.

"Who?" asked Lo.

"The one who took my gun, that's the boy who used to hang out at your place in Bannack in his gray Secesh uniform."

"You sure?"

"Damn sure," said Jane.

"No more Faro for him," Lo said.

"We should tell somebody."

"Tell who?"

Jane thought about that for a moment. "Tell somebody. Leastwise he could be watched."

"No. Better tell no one," Lo said. "We tell, he know we tell. Better keep quiet."

"How is anybody ever going to get rid of these bandits if no one even talks?" Jane protested.

"Get rich, get out, they say," said Lo. "Get rich, get out best for Lo."

"That may be good for you, but what about me?" asked Jane.

Lo paused. Didn't seem to have a good answer for that one. "You good partner. We good partners, no?"

"That we are, anyhow. We're bang-up good partners, Lo," she said.

As Lo climbed onto his steed, he added: "Calamity Jane not with Lo, bang, bandits shoot Lo dead. Bang, Lo dead. We good partners."

Jane and Lo arrived in town just as the sun was setting. At Madam Chi's, Jane gave Lo the bag of gold she'd hid and they parted ways. Jane proceeded on foot, after giving her pony a good pat on the neck and receiving a nuzzle in return. At home, Ma gave her a hug which she barely resisted, and Pa raised himself from bed onto his elbow. Lana rejoiced to see her older sister and wanted to know all about the stampede.

Jane told the story in glorious detail—leaving out the part about the robbery on the return trip, of course. She didn't want her folks trying to prevent her return because of the danger. Lana was enthralled by Jane's description of the noisy, dusty rush to Alder: the horde of men, the miner's meeting, and especially the mad rush at the end where everybody dropped their pots and pans, bedrolls, tents, and all to make the final dash for a claim. Lana wanted to know: why would everyone drop all that valuable stuff? And why hadn't Jane staked a claim herself, especially since all she would have had to do was pound a stake in the ground?

Over the next few days the majority of the skeptics, as well as Jane's friends, packed up and made their way to the new diggings. The Canarys occupied a near ghost town, while Pa slowly recuperated. One morning Jane awoke to the sound of snorting horses and Lo's terse speech pattern outside the cabin. She pulled on her clothes quickly and went outside. There was a wagon loaded with items from Madam Chi's saloon, with Madam Chi riding in front, and Lo riding Black Bess. He held her saddled pony's halter in his hand.

"Good morning, Jane," Lo said.

Pa sat on a crate, propped against the cabin's outside wall. In his hand, he gently twisted a small buckskin pouch. He called Jane to his side. "There ain't nothin' like near dying to focus the mind, girl. Makes a body rethink his priorities. You doin' okay?" Pa was still awfully weak, but also more calm and focused than she had seen in a long time. Jane looked at the buckskin pouch. Pa held it up. "And then there is this. I'll take it, but it ain't right, that this family has to depend on you.

You are gonna see a changed man now, I promise." He tousled her hair.
"We'll follow soon," Pa said to Lo. "I can't ride a horse yet, but soon I could tolerate my carcass being hauled in a wagon."

Jane hugged Ma, hugged Lana longer, then jumped on her pony, and with a wave to her family, she and Lo followed the lumbering wagon.

There was no need to worry about being robbed on the return trip to Alder, as any bandit would not expect them to carry gold in this direction. The trip went uneventfully, but when they came within sight of the new gold camp, the place was nearly unrecognizable. The entire near side of the stream had been burned clear of brush, alder trees and all, and piles of burned tents and equipment lay about. Fortunately, the far side of the gulch, including Lo's rustic emporium, had been untouched by flames. A miner's meeting was underway, attended by everyone within sight. At the center of the crowd was a wagon, on which stood Mr. Fergus and a man in a fine striped coat whom Jane had seen around here and there in Bannack.

Lo motioned to the crowd. "No Faro now—all busy miner's meeting. I take pony. You come after meeting."

It was true that there was no gambling in town at the moment, but the river of whiskey that always flowed to the populace continued unchecked. Skinner and the rest of Lo's competitors sod whiskey at plank bars at the periphery of the meeting. Whiskey that went by names like Forty Rod, Sudden Death, Tanglefoot and Tarantula Juice been taken in restrained fashion in Bannack by comparison to this scene.

Jane waved to Andrew, James, and Robert, who watched the proceedings from a comfortable distance on a nearby knoll. She approached the boys. "Hey Andrew. What's the deal with the fire?"

"Some drunk idiots didn't put out their campfire," he replied. "Wind came up the gulch and it was near like a chimney." He indicated the miner's court in progress. "They just finished setting up a buddy system so's the miners that were on the other side share with the ones that lost their gear."

"What's your Pa doing?"

"They appointed him judge," said Andrew, with obvious pride. "My Dad's the smartest man this side of Pike's Peak."

"Don't say," Jane said. Andrew usually seemed awkward and hesitant around his Pa, but he sure swelled with pride now.

Jane greeted Robert, who seemed to be trying to ignore her. "That your wagon?" she asked, pointing to Mr. Fergus' perch.

"Yeah," said Robert, disdainfully.

Jane shook her head slightly and leaned in toward James. "Your brother born with a broomstick up his butt like that, or is this something he has to cultivate?" "Cultivate" was a big word Jane had learned around the Faro tables. James coughed and laughed simultaneously so hard he almost fell over. "There, there, son," said Jane, clapping his back. "Breathe first, THEN swallow your spit, separate like. You should practice that." Robert hadn't heard what Jane said and he waved her away, then bent over to see what was wrong with his brother.

Jane turned her attention to the proceedings before them. The final details were completed in the matter of the fire. Next, initial arguments were made in a case of infringement of one sort or another between adjacent claims. It turned out that the man in the striped suit was a lawyer by the name of Smith, who made arguments for one side while the other side made their own case without the benefit of legal counsel.

Many in the crowd were inebriated to the point that the finer points of legal arguments were completely wasted on their muddled minds. Mr. Fergus was doing his dignified best to see that the arguments of both sides were given appropriate airing for the more sober individuals present. Working against his attempt to look the part of judge was that hat, way too small for his learned head and looking like a jester's cap with tufts of his untrimmed hair jutting out from the slashes in it. The contrast between the judge's somber attitude and his comical appearance was an opportunity for his ever-present friends to rib him. At every opportunity, they would chime in, "Oh, most wise, Judge," or some such exclamation.

This jesting came to a climax when lawyer Smith called for a "motion for nonsuit." Mr. Fergus fell silent, and his serious demeanor took on a befuddled tinge. Jane took that look to mean that Judge Fergus, learned though he was, did not understand what a motion for nonsuit meant. His friends, apparently having come to the same conclusion, waited with bated laughter to see how His Honor would extricate himself from the situation without damaging his dignity in the eyes of the entire community. Fergus pondered his predicament as his friends poked each other playfully. He glanced sourly at lawyer Smith for having purposely put him in this awkward position, then examined his palms with furrowed brow, as if the answer might be somewhere in his own grasp. Suddenly, his face brightened, and he once again assumed his magisterial demeanor. "A nonsuit, eh? On what grounds?" he asked.

Mr. Fergus' friends called out again with great mirth, "Solomon himself would envy this man," and so forth. They clapped each other on their backs and laughed at how cleverly the judge had extricated himself from his predicament. Smith explained that "nonsuit" meant that the case should be thrown out for total lack of merit, and Judge Fergus was able to rule that such a motion would obviously be inappropriate in this situation, to the satisfaction of the crowd, and to the mirth of his friends.

Jane turned to Andrew and said with more than grudging admiration, "Your Pa is a clever man."

Andrew hadn't seemed to catch the significance of the nonsuit issue, but at Jane's praise he beamed proudly. Arguments in the case came to a close, and Judge Fergus put it to a vote. Miners shouted "aye" and "nay" to the motion at hand, and it seemed obvious to Jane which side had won. However, the losing side didn't see it that way and contested the ruling—or at least, one of their number did. This bear-like man was among the more inebriated men present, and thus disinhibited, he began to make threats directed at the other litigants. Judge Fergus attempted to quell this by defending the legitimacy of the ruling, which only served to draw the man's attention more specifically to him. As the drunk swayed and shouted epithets in all directions, he clumsily drew his revolver. The crowd fell away, which further emboldened him. Jane tensed up, and she could feel Andrew trembling next to her. She wanted to reassure her friend, but had she done so, it would have been empty sentiment. This was a dangerous situation, and all present knew it. The crowd's shouting changed to urgent murmuring as the man's partners attempted to mollify him, but he only pointed his gun at them as well as he twirled in a stumbling crouch.

Suddenly, a man stepped out of the crowd and, by his bold demeanor, took command of the situation. It was Plummer. The attention of the entire crowd of hundreds was suddenly riveted on him.

"That's the end of this," said Plummer to the big man.

"What the hell do you care, Plummer?" replied the drunk.

"This is a miner's court. There was a fair vote, and the matter is finished," said Plummer. Even a

drunk man could see from Plummer's slight crouch and rotation of form that he was ready for a gunfight. "You should apologize to the judge for your behavior, don't you think?"

This took the wind out of the man's sails, but any outcome was still possible. Seconds seemed to drag like minutes, but finally he cracked a smile and fumbled to tuck his weapon in his belt. His partners crowded around him and tried to hurry him away, but huge man that he was, he shook them loose.

"No, no, Plummer is right. I want to 'pologize to the judge," he slurred. "Cap'n," he said, nearly missing his forehead with an inebriated salute, "I'm damn sorry, and I hope you will forgive my bad manners." He then sought out the nearest of his opposing litigants, whom he gave a big hug. Then, he invited

all of them to the closest plank bar for reparative drinks, which they accepted.

The crowd's reaction was mixed to this show of apology by a man who had endangered them all, but Mr. Fergus was of the mind that no crisis should go wasted.

"Fellow citizens," he shouted. "I present to you that this community has gone too long without a sheriff. Mr. Fairweather, do you agree?"

"No argument from me on that one," Fairweather said.

"I will then take nominations for Sheriff of Alder," shouted Mr. Fergus above the noise of the crowd. "I am looking for a brave, sober man of good moral character."

There was a pause as the men of Alder scanned the faces of their fellow citizens.

"The 'sober' part limits the field pretty severely," said Edgar, to laughter.

"I nominate Henry Plummer!" a voice called out.

"Henry Plummer, so noted," said Fergus. "Do we have any other nominations?"

The crowd fell silent. Fergus searched faces in the crowd. "Any other nominations, then?"

Into the silence, Plummer interjected, "It takes a man of fortitude and determination to be Sheriff in a place like this. I think I am that man."

"Vote! Vote!" came the cry from the crowd.

Mr. Fergus put the question to a vote. "All that say we elect Henry Plummer as Sheriff, say 'aye.' "

A rumbling of "ayes" rolled through the crowd.

"All those opposed, say, 'nay,' " Fergus called. Here and there a "nay" vote was called out.

"Then so be it," Fergus shouted. "Mr. Plummer, you are our new sheriff!"

"Hmm," Jane said to Andrew. "Things are looking up!"

Chapter 10

Day by day, more men poured into Alder, as news of the richness of the discovery spread rapidly. Men from all across the West made tracks for the new El Dorado as the news reached them, and every day dozens arrived. None were disappointed. Newly constructed sluice boxes yielded phenomenal amounts of gold on some claims, and the poorest claim still yielded double what the average claim back in Bannack had. In the span of a few weeks, the men who had arrived with the initial stampede, including those who had been burned out in the brush fire, were wealthier than they had ever dreamed possible. Every square foot along Alder Creek's fourteen-mile length that wasn't bare rock had been staked within the first few weeks, and the men now pouring in from all over the West either bought a claim or worked for the early arrivals in one way or another.

Day by day Jane dealt Faro to these raucous miners while the new camp took shape around her, and she made good money doing so. Lo no longer had to make the dangerous trip to Bannack, as the big supply wagons passed through that nearly deserted town and went on to Alder. Pa recovered enough to load up on one of these lumbering conveyances, and made the trip with Ma and Lana. The Alder that Jane's family saw when they arrived bore absolutely no resemblance to the wilderness on which Jane had first laid eyes. A main street of tent and lean-to businesses, a full third of which were saloons, overlooked a streambed of teeming activity. One could scarcely see stable ground on either side of the creek, as it was constantly being shoveled and carried to sluice boxes by whole armies of sweating, grunting, cursing men. The Canary family set up housekeeping in this hive of activity in a simple lean-to, and Ma set to her business of laundering. Newly sober Pa had arrived too late to stake a claim, so he swallowed his pride and found a job sawing lumber.

But all was not well in Alder. Around Jane's Faro table there was frequently dark conversation alluding to robberies and men who went missing. Jane felt burdened by her knowledge and suspicions of the culprits every time she overheard such talk. As the tales of mayhem and robbery increased, her conscience gnawed away at her. Finally, she decided to confide in the one man in town who was now charged with law and order in the new gold camp.

Plummer was known to take target practice out in back of the blacksmith shop from time to time, sometimes showing off his skill to an audience, sometimes alone. One day, on her way to Lo's place, Jane saw him, this time alone. She circled around so he would see her approach. Seemed wise to not startle a man in the midst of target practice.

"Howdy, Miss Calamity," he said.

They had never met, but it was no surprise that he would know the most popular Faro dealer in camp on sight. "Morning, Sheriff," she said.

"I hear you are pretty good with a rifle," he said, as he loaded his gun.

"I could pick fleas off'n my dog from fifty yards, if she would stop scratching," she said.

"You ever shoot one of these?" he asked, holding out his well-oiled Navy revolver for Jane to see.

"Ain't so much as held one."

"Here, then," he said as he handed her the sleek gun.

The barrel of the gun felt warm in her left hand from recent firing, the handle smooth and natural in her right.

"Got a nice balance to it," she said.

"Go ahead, then."

"You sure?" she asked.

"Sure. Try that post there."

Jane carefully drew a bead and fired. Dirt spat up in front of the post.

"A bit heavy for you, I suppose," said Plummer. "Practice with your rifle one-handed some, then come by and try again some time."

"I wish I could return the favor," Jane said.

"You might, someday," said Plummer. "A Sheriff can't be everywhere at once. I could use your eyes and ears."

"That's what I came about, anyhow," said Jane. "Maybe I recognized a bandit that robbed us."

"Who is 'us'?" he asked.

"Me and the Chinaman." Lo was still the only Chinaman in Alder.

"Go on."

"You know this character that used to wear a Southern uniform, got a gimpy left leg?"

"I know him."

"He's one."

"Could you tell any of the others?"

"Nah, just him."

"You told anyone else?" Plummer asked.

"Nah."

"I'll keep an eye on him, then," said Plummer. "Thanks for that. You keep me informed, Jane."

He took back his revolver with his left hand, and cradled it in his right, which Jane had never noted before, but it was severely clawed and almost useless.

"What happened to your hand?" she asked.

"Gunfight in Bannack. My opponent didn't take the same view as myself as to what constituted a fair fight, and he took a potshot at me."

"At least you didn't lose the arm."

"Dr. Glick saved my arm," he said.

"Huh!" she said. "Glick ever say anything to you about the bandits around here?"

"Dr. Glick and I are well acquainted," he said. "Just spoke to him yesterday. But this topic has never come up."

Something about that seemed odd to Jane. Was Glick so afraid of the bandits that he would not even hint to Plummer what he knew? "Well, you should ask him some time."

"I'll do that then, next we meet," Plummer said.

"Thanks for the pistol lesson."

"My pleasure."

"You'll watch out for that fellow?" Jane asked.

"Will do," said Plummer. "And if you see anything else suspicious, you will tell me first?"

"Sure," said Jane.

"Oh, and best to keep this just between us, right?" said Plummer. "I know this fellow's sort, and it's best, for now."

Just as in Bannack, Monday through Saturday entailed backbreaking work from dawn to dusk for miners. Late Saturday on every claim, the partners would divide the week's gold amongst themselves and go to bed early. Then the next morning the typical miner, who had barely left the narrow confines of his claim all week, would take his gold poke and head into town. There he would wander from saloon to saloon for a time, then on to a dance hall to buy a dance with a stout-framed German girl or two, and maybe seek momentary pleasure in the arms of a prostitute. He would gamble at poker or a Faro table, or bet on a boxing match or a horse race. All this was lubricated with alcohol. At the end of the day he would return to his claim, most often with an empty gold poke, to start the weekly cycle all over again the following day.

Pa, now that he was a reformed man, steered clear of the Sunday bacchanal both to avoid the temptation of drink and at the same time, to save money. There were other sensible-minded men like him, but they were in the minority. Most of the camp, now numbering more than a thousand, crowded into Main Street every Sunday.

Jane also worked Monday through Friday at the Faro table. It was fun—not hardly the backbreaking work of a miner, nor a sawyer like Pa, but work still. She also helped Ma with laundry every Saturday, which was certainly work. So on Sunday, Jane headed to town with all the rest, eager for excitement and to blow off steam. One such Sunday, after helping Ma with breakfast cleanup and saying goodbye to Lana and Pa, Jane headed out. She and Andrew usually met at the horse races, and this was her ultimate destination this Sunday.

From her doorway, the town sounded like a roaring waterfall, a veritable Niagara of celebration and activity, nearly drowning out the sound of the occasional gunshot. She passed through the burned-out part of town, the doused campfire smell of it still faintly discernible. She trotted past the idle sluices and panted as she hopped across the log bridge that crossed Alder Creek, so similar to Bannack. Alder was maturing from a mining camp to a mining town. Kustar's bakery stood before her, the first log structure in town, and there were a few other log buildings in various stages of construction, but most of the town was still comprised of brush lean-tos and tents. A tumultuous crowd milled about Main Street, moving in and out of saloons, dance halls, and such.

Jane eyed three mounted Indian braves conversing with a half-Indian fellow she had seen around town. She must have stared at the little group for too long, for one of the Indians turned his horse her way, erect and proud as he approached. He had the look of a warrior, armed only with a knife at his waist, a mixture of dignity and ferocity in equal parts. He pulled his horse to a halt, raised his chin, and pointed to his chest. "Me," he said with a pause, "Clark." Having seemingly exhausted his English, he nodded to Jane and sauntered away, collecting the other two braves as he did, and they continued up the street.

The half-Indian smiled at Jane's perplexity and approached her. "My name is John Innis," he said.

"I know you," said Jane. "They say you are a first-rate tracker. They call me Calamity Jane."

"Pleased to make your acquaintance, Calamity. The Indian brave wanted to tell you that his father was Clark, the explorer," said Innis.

Jane's eyes went wide. "Of Lewis and Clark?"

Innis nodded. "He's the only blue-eyed Indian I ever met."

"No way!" Jane said. "Lewis and Clark!" What a thrill to meet a living legacy of those great men, the first white men to set eyes on this area. Innis laughed and took his leave of Jane, who proceeded uphill on Main Street. The further she went, the more she became engulfed in the circus-like atmosphere of a Sunday in a gold camp. The saloons, some wood structures, some tents were all full, and from within were heard the songs of carousing men, the clinking of glasses, and the clicking of poker chips. A man led a mule up the street, shouting at the top of his lungs. "Sale or trade! Sturdiest beast you will ever see. Sale or trade!" More mangy than sturdy, thought Jane; it only served to remind her that her goal was the horse races. She pressed on.

A wagon passed carrying Fairweather and Edgar, along with a couple of their buddies and a bevy of dance hall girls and gaudily dressed prostitutes—all singing and waving champagne bottles in the air. Edgar beckoned Jane to climb on board, but she was not interested in the company of drunk adults.

Further up the street was a Jewish peddler, hawking his wares. "Red flannel shirts! Finest material!" he shouted. Competing with him for attention across the way was a preacher, thumping his Bible forcefully at the jeering crowd gathered around him. "Gather 'round, sinners, come hear the word of the Lord for your eternal salvation. I turn to Revelation twenty, verse ten, and I quote, 'And the devil who deceived them was thrown into the lake of fire and brimstone, where the beast and the false prophet are also; and they will be tormented day and night forever and ever.' Be this a warning to all of you..."

"Oh, save me, Preacher," cried Edgar in exaggerated jest from his perch on the wagon, "for I have sinned!" He grabbed one of the bawdy women at his side, kissed her lewdly, and fondled her breasts to laughter and cheers from the men.

"Ignore the word of the Lord at your own eternal peril," thundered the preacher, "you who give no thought to tomorrow, you who ignore the evil around you and instead worship the golden calf and seek the transitory pleasures of the flesh." His voice was powerful, and he meant what he said. "A day of reckoning is coming for all of us. Will you stand before your maker with a clean conscience?" The crowd was silenced for a moment by the preacher's force.

"Red flannel shirts. Two dollars. Highest quality fabric," cried the peddler. "Buy a warm shirt today. Worry about Hell tomorrow."

The crowd laughed, and Jane continued up the street. She spied a scantily dressed woman smoking a cigarette outside a tent, who returned her look with haughty good humor. Not everybody took the day off. Jane didn't think any less of this woman for her chosen profession. She wasn't anyone's mother.

Attracted by waves of shouts and cheers, Jane peered between two saloon tents and glimpsed a fistfight that was just getting underway. The two combatants were stripped to the waist and circled each other warily while agitated patrons shouted and bet on the outcome. Jane watched for a few minutes, enthralled by the force of the blows the men inflicted upon one another, but the boxers moved out of her narrow view, so she moved on. She quickened her pace towards the horse racing underway just ahead, where she spotted Andrew and friends James, Robert, and Dez.

Andrew waved Jane toward them.

"Hey," Jane greeted them.

"You gotta see this," Andrew said.

"Hey, Jane," said James. Robert gave her a disdainful glance.

"Hey, James. Dez," said Jane.

Jane was too short to see what was going on from where they stood. "Come on," she said to Andrew, who was barely taller than her. They pushed their way through to the front of the crowd. What they

saw was a race in progress, but what a contest! Rather than the usual horse race, this was a fellow on foot racing a horse and rider on a course between two poles only about thirty yards apart. The contest was in full swing, the man sweating profusely and responding with a grin to the cheers that arose from the crowd every time he rounded a corner. Edgar, Fairweather, their cronies, and their girls cheered from the wagon. Clark, the Indian, and his cohorts watched impassively from the periphery on their horses, while the rest of the crowd surged and seethed on foot.

The race was evenly matched. The horse was a beautiful, graceful Sorrel mare, which passed the man on the straightaway on each lap, but humanity's entrant in the contest caught up each time the horse made its awkward corner turn. Jane and Andrew rooted for the two-legged sprinter, as did most. A gun was fired: last lap. Horse and man had traded the lead on every lap, but in the homestretch of the final lap, the mare did not need to slow down to corner and easily galloped across the finish line ahead of her bipedal foe. The man's friends rushed to his side and clapped him on the back as he crouched and panted. He smiled through his abating exhaustion as his friends consoled him in German and helped him limp off. "Beer" sounds the same in German and English, and Jane surmised that they intended to salve their wounded pride with a frothy brew or two.

Jane was disappointed that the German fellow had lost, but she did admire the horse. Who owned this magnificent Sorrel steed? The rider dismounted and led the horse to Plummer, who was collecting bets from Fairweather and the rest.

"Any more takers?" called Plummer. "Who thinks they can outrace my horse?"

Robert, James, and Dez rejoined Jane and Andrew. The crowd milled about, waiting to see if there would be another challenger.

"That's a beautiful horse," Robert said to Dez.

Jane found herself envious of Dez's beauty, of how Robert wanted to talk to Dez and ignored her. Envious, despite how Robert was something of a jerk. "Nah, I could beat that nag," she said.

James straightened up with eyes wide. "No way!"

"Sure," Jane said, with her usual cocky manner. "I could beat her easy."

"Let's go, then," said Robert.

Second thoughts crossed Jane's mind for a moment, but there was no turning back now, and besides, here was a challenge worthy of her intrepid spirit, a way to prove herself to her friends. Robert led the four of them towards Plummer and his men, wending their way through the crowd, which had broken up into smaller groups of men, boasting and bantering amongst themselves. The little group of friends approached Plummer and his men. Robert puffed up his chest, and with a firm voice said, "Excuse me."

The men seemed not to notice.

"Excuse me," said Robert.

Still no response. Plummer was picking through gold nuggets offered by Fairweather and Edgar, ignoring Jane and friends.

"Hey, Sheriff," said Dez. "We want to race your horse."

"Oh, you do, now, do you?" he said.

Andrew pressed their cause. "Jane can beat your stupid horse any day!"

"Jane?" said Plummer. "My friend Calamity Jane?"

"Hey Plummer, give her a chance. I want to make my money back," Edgar said.

"Yeah, Plummer, give the kids a chance," chimed in a woman on the wagon.

"I'm all for it," said Plummer. "Ladies and gentlemen, we have a challenger! The girl known far and wide as Calamity Jane will take on my humble steed. I am giving three-to-one odds. Do I have any takers?"

Jane knew the answer to that question, having watched these men at her Faro table now for months. When at their leisure, they would bet on anything that moved; or if it didn't move they might bet on when it might. Bettors nearly attacked Plummer for the chance at this action. Among them was Cecil and his partner from the Solomon Islands. After placing his bet, Cecil said, "I got money on you, Missy," with his usual big grin and a wink. His partner from the Solomon Islands smiled at her and licked his lips.

"Tell your partner he can eat the loser," she said.

Cecil laughed.

The friends huddled. "Listen," Jane said to James, "I got an idea. But I need your gloves."

James turned to run, but Robert grabbed his arm. "Hey. That's the only pair we have," he said.

"Oh, for goodness sake, Robert," said Dez. "She can't wear them out racing a horse."

Robert looked chastised, and James took off for home.

Jane sized up the rider, who gave her a nasty look in return. He swung up on Plummer's horse. Plummer announced that he had taken all the bets that he could afford, turning some away disappointed. Besides the bets Plummer took, there were innumerable side bets among friends and acquaintances. One of the Indians pointed to Jane, then indicated a bracelet he wore and the other brave's breastplate. The other agreed silently and turned to the son of Clark, who nodded his agreement to bear witness to their bet.

James returned with the gloves as the course was being cleared of spectators, and Jane put them on. Plummer drew a starting line in the dirt with the heel of his boot. He eyed Jane's gloves. "You aren't planning to grab on to her tail and skid the whole course, are you?" he said.

"Just watch and see," Jane said, and put her left foot on the starting line in a sideways crouch.

Plummer pulled out his big Navy revolver. He watched his horse prance as the rider positioned her. "The race is five laps," he said. "For the starting gun, it's one, two, 'bang,' and off you go. Got it?"

Jane nodded.

Plummer positioned himself close behind Jane, where she couldn't see him. "One... two..." BANG!

The loudness of the fired gun, scant feet behind Jane, caused her legs to jump reflexively. She took a step forward and stumbled. If she had fallen flat, that might have been the end of the race. But she'd learned another thing from her Pa back in Missouri, and that was how to roll whenever you fall. When she first stumbled, a low rumble of dismay came from the crowd. When she rolled over her shoulder and was back up on her feet in the blink of an eye, the rumble turned to cheers. She had lost ground that would be hard to regain, but she was still in the race. The majority of the shouting mass of men was rooting for her in the first place, and after that bit of acrobatics even most of the ones who had bet against her cheered her on. Thus encouraged, she dug in with intensity.

As was to be expected, the mare arrived at the pole first, but had to be brought to a near stop as she turned. Even so she was past the pole by the time Jane came abreast of it. The gloves now came into use. When Jane was almost even with the pole, she reached out and grabbed it with her left hand (as the race was going counterclockwise around the poles) and pulled herself around in a tight cornering maneuver, which caused her to accelerate. The men in the crowd hooted and cheered at this tactic, which brought Jane even with the horse's hindquarters. Again the Sorrel gained on the straightaway, and the crowd noise died down. Again Jane spun around on the pole, this time more gracefully, and it appeared that she was gaining ground. She saw the rider look back at her, menacingly, after this turn. Again the horse gained on her on the straightaway. This time, though, the rider guided the horse to turn farther beyond the pole, which lost horse and rider time, but when the Sorrel charged back to the pole she was at nearly full speed, and the rider maneuvered so there was no room between the horse and the pole. As a result, Jane had to wait for the horse to pass, then swing around the pole, which slowed the momentum she gained from the pole-grabbing maneuver. She repeated this for one more lap, looking for an opening, but found none. She was too far behind.

A stratagem occurred to Jane as she struggled for breath. Was this the corner to use it, or should she wait? She thought it best to run this lap and examine the course with her new ploy in mind. That would only leave the gun lap. She would have no chance to make up the distance between her and her equine foe if her idea failed. She ran a lap, examining closely the timing of how her opponent cornered. Plummer fired his gun in the air. Last lap. Jane used all her remaining strength to keep the horse's straightaway gain to a minimum. She approached the pole with all possible speed, knowing that to slip and fall again would mean she would certainly lose and possibly be trampled. After the mare passed the pole and turned to face her, Jane made a sideways move to the opposite side of the pole, flung both arms out, and shouted. This was just as the mare started her charge towards the pole. The mare, faced unexpectedly with a girl directly in front of her, arms flailing and shouting, was startled and reared up slightly. That was all Jane needed. She grabbed the pole with her right hand and swung around it in the opposite direction. She was now ahead of the mare by two full lengths. Jane put every ounce of effort she had left into the last straightaway sprint. The rider spurred the mare on and slapped her hindquarters with a switch. The horse accelerated and narrowed the gap, but couldn't close it. Jane's lead was just too much for horse and rider to erase. Jane crossed the finish line a horse's neck ahead of the Sorrel, grinning and panting, with arms raised in victory.

Andrew met Jane at the finish line, hugged her, and clapped her on the back. Cecil and Edgar raised her on their shoulders and paraded her around to the cheers of all. Jane bathed in the men's adulation with a big grin as she bounced around on their shoulders, smiling and waving.

Plummer shook his head and looked at the ground. He held his arms in the air and shouted for quiet. "Now, now, fair is fair. A horse race is run in a circle, not a damn figure eight. That whole last gambit reeks. All bets are off. I'm refunding all bets."

Cecil and Edgar put Jane down gently and joined in the roars of disapproval and laughter from the crowd. "Now see here, Plummer," Edgar called out. "You got beat by a girl. And you are so much more the loser if you don't admit it."

One of the dance hall girls chimed in, "She's a little girl, Plummer, for God's sakes!" This assertion resonated with the crowd, which voiced unanimous agreement.

Plummer put his hands on his hips with his head down for a moment. He held his arms up again and waited for silence. "I am first and foremost a fair man," said Plummer. "I believe that the rule of law and keeping one's word is what sets us apart from the savages."

The Indians, still watching impassively, showed no reaction, whether they understood the reference to them or not.

Plummer continued, "I am also a public servant now and perhaps I should bow to the will of the people. I will pay all bets in full."

The crowd approved, and men crowded around Plummer for their three-to-one payout.

Andrew clapped Jane on her back. She removed her gloves and held them out for Robert, but it was James who took them from her. Dez gave her an exuberant hug.

The two Indians who had made their side bet turned to the son of Clark, who indicated that the breastplate be given to the brave who had bet on Jane. That item was surrendered, and after the winning bettor had adjusted the trophy on his chest to his full satisfaction, the trio sauntered off.

Jane had never been so happy and carefree in all her life as in the weeks following the horse race. She strode about town with the confidence that she belonged here as much as she ever had belonged in the wilderness, and she was greeted on the street by men as a celebrity of sorts. They came to her Faro table just to banter with her and recount over and over how she had outwitted horse and rider. The numerous players around her faro table bought her pastries and coffee at her slightest whim and generally treated her like one of them. Cecil came down from his claim now and then to share in this, and judging by how he bet, he had found a rich claim up there. Madam Chi raised Jane's pay, and Greaseball found some other place to haunt with his disgusting leer. It was all so much fun that Jane mostly lost contact with her friends. They spent a lot of their time going to school anyhow, but even so, Jane found her celebrity among grown men more enticing than her friendship with her peers, and so she spent more and more time at the Faro tables.

Jane was on the upswing, but the town was on a downswing. Gone was the giddy impermanence of a camp, as most of the tent structures were replaced by more sturdy wooden ones, and the number of new arrivals in town tapered off. The general exuberance faded and was tempered by the approach of winter. The bets became more restrained at Jane's Faro table, the banter less playful. Great wealth had been extracted from Alder Creek, but soon the temperature would dip below freezing and no more gold would be produced until spring. Fairweather and Edgar still had more money than they knew what to do with. They loved to show their good fortune by buying rounds of drinks and food for all the men in whichever saloon they found themselves, upon any whim that blew their way. Similarly wealthy was anyone who had been on the initial stampede, but some of the new arrivals took on the role of "bummers" and spent a lot of time hanging around the saloons just to benefit from the generosity of wealthier men.

Alder Creek itself was a scene of environmental pillage. There was no vegetation within thirty yards on either side of it for the fourteen miles it traversed from high in the mountains near Cecil's claim to its terminus at the Beaverhead River. Hired men trampled and shoveled its banks in ceaseless activity from dawn to dusk, Monday through Saturday. Nobody referred to Alder Creek anymore; it was now Alder Gulch, a guttural, unpleasant appellation that in a monosyllabic grunt described the devastation men had wreaked upon the pristine wilderness.

It wasn't only the approach of winter that dampened the mood; Jane continued to hear muttered talk of the ongoing crime spree on the trails around town. Tales of narrow escapes from bandits, and the rising count of men who had seemed to disappear, were circulated in hushed tones. Though Alder had a sheriff now, it didn't seem that things were any better than they had been in Bannack. Jane kept what she knew to herself as these tales circulated around her table, for what else could she do?

One crisp autumn afternoon Jane took her leave from Madam Chi's after receiving her pay. She headed toward her friend Ezekial's store to buy items Ma had specified that morning. But she lost the bounce in her step when an old acquaintance exited the store, a sack of goods on his shoulder. It was her ex-patient, Lefty. He spotted her as well and gave a knowing smile.

"Calamity," he said, "if I be friend enough to call you that."

"Lefty. Long time," she replied.

"Lotta water under the bridge since I last set eyes on you."

"Where you been hiding?" Jane asked. She scanned the streets for Plummer.

"You don't think I would actually tell you, now, do you?" he asked.

"No, don't reckon so," she said. "How's yer arm?"

"I was hopin' for better, last time we met. Every time he shifted his load, Lefty winced in pain. Warn't your fault none. Y'all done a fine job." He was wearing a fancy gambler's tie around his neck, incongruous with the rest of his rough appearance. Jane imagined him putting it on that morning for his first visit to town in months.

"How do you get that thing around your neck, anyhow?" she asked.

Lefty smiled. "You are a smart one, girl. I tie it over a post and then sling it over my neck. Gotta look respectable."

"You worried they might sling something else around your neck, now that they got a Sheriff?" Jane asked.

"Sheriff, huh," Lefty laughed. He shifted his load and winced again. "I hear you beat my buddy Plummer's horse," he said.

"It's still a small town, if word got to you," said Jane.

Lefty's face softened and he looked her in the eye. "I also hear you been doin' okay for yourself."

"Can't complain."

"If you want any advice from the likes of me, it's this: be careful who you trust, and same as that, be careful what crowd you fall in with. I might not be in the mess I'm in if I had thought twice on that." The curtain fell on his moment of kindness and concern, and his face hardened. Wordlessly he strode past her, as if they had never met.

Jane watched him go until he was out of sight, then ran to the shooting range that Plummer frequented. Plummer was there, she was relieved to see, with his back to her in a shooting contest with another man.

"Sheriff," she called.

"Calamity, my dear," called out the lawman.

"Remember what you told me about bein' your eyes and ears?"

"Sure do."

Jane was about to spill her tale about Lefty and how he got shot, and tell Plummer that the villain now could be followed to his hideout, when the other man turned around. It was Greaseball.

"Yes?" asked Plummer. It seemed like she had interrupted a moment of camaraderie between these two men.

Jane was too startled to speak for a moment. But then a realization struck her like lightning. Plummer was the missing piece of the puzzle. She regained her balance quickly. "I heard someone's claim been jumped," said Jane. "Up towards Summit."

"If that's so," said Plummer, "and if the varmints survive until Sunday, I'm sure the boys will make their case in miner's court. I don't have jurisdiction until then."

"Sure," said Jane. "My mistake then."

"Well, thanks then," said Plummer. "You keep up the good work."

"Yeah, I will," said Jane. "Your eyes and ears, Sheriff." Greaseball smirked at her as she turned to go. She was tired of that look. She was tired of him, period, and now she was mad at Plummer, too. "Oh yeah, Sheriff, met a buddy of yours today. Bum arm. Seems like he wished he'd never met a varmint like you."

"Why Jane, I'm surprised at you," said Plummer in measured cadence. "You should show your elders more respect."

"I do, them what deserves it," she said. Betrayal ached in Jane's mind. "What the hell makes you who you are, Plummer?" she blurted.

Plummer examined the charges in his gun. "I don't know what you think you know, darlin', but let me tell you a story. It's the story of a sheriff in California. Damn good sheriff, risked his life more than once to bring dangerous men in for trial. But one time, he killed a low-life wife-beater when the scumbag had already drawn a bead on him. Good folks in town, they had a trial. That sheriff went to prison.

Prison. Nearly died there, abandoned by all the good people he had protected.".

"So what, this storybook sheriff made new friends in prison?" Jane asked.

Plummer fixed Jane with a cold hard stare. "I was born to lead, my dear. Ever since I can remember, those around me turned to me to lead. Anyhow, best for you to be careful about what you think know, missy, and who you tell what." Plummer gave Greaseball a glance.

"Whore's spawn," Greaseball sneered.

Anger boiled in Jane, but she checked it. Ignoring Greaseball, she said to Plummer, "Look at you, master of all you survey, thinkin' hell would freeze over before anyone would suspect you or listen to me. Well, I ain't but a kid, but far as I can see, life is full of surprises, mister." With that, Jane took her leave.

Chapter 11

A sense of unease fell over Jane's world in the days after that meeting with Plummer. She wanted to talk her suspicions out with someone, but with whom? Her parents? She could only see them treating her like a child if she told them. Same for Mr. Fergus. Andrew? They hadn't seen each other much lately, and what could a kid do? Dr. Glick? Seemed he already knew but was afraid for his life; hadn't he referred to previously meeting the "boss" when he patched up Lefty? Ben Ezekial? No, she wanted to confide in the one adult who treated her as an equal.

So one morning, Jane walked into Madam Chi's to seek him out. The place was called Madam Chi's again ever since they moved out of Lo's bower and into a more substantial wooden structure. Jane was about to push past the familiar Bengal Tiger sign when she heard a gunshot. Seemed to come from further up the street, away from the saloons. No matter.

"Miss Calamity," Chi said with a deep bow, "welcome."

Jane bowed.

"You come," said Chi, motioning Jane outside.

"Where is Lo?" Jane asked.

"Come see first," Chi said. She led Jane toward the rear of the saloon. As they rounded the back corner, Jane saw a rope tethered to a post, and a few steps on saw Lightning pawing the ground.

"You take," said Chi.

Jane went wide-eyed when she realized Chi was giving her the pony. She whirled around and gave her a big hug, which the Madam took awkwardly.

"Jane's pony now. You earn pony," said Chi.

"But where will I keep him?" Jane asked.

"Stables, same as before. Lo pay."

"Okay, but where is Lo?" Jane asked.

"Lo good friend Jane," said Chi.

"Sure," said Jane.

"Lo not want to say good-bye," said Chi.

"What?" Jane said.

"You tell no one." She leaned close to Jane. "Lo go San Francisco. Yesterday."

Jane's face dropped. Her best friend in the world hadn't trusted her enough to say good-bye. "I wish he was here to thank," she mumbled.

"You still keep secret," said Chi.

Jane hopped up on Lightning. "Is he coming back?"

"Maybe springtime," Chi said. "Lo sorry, not want risk tell anyone he leaving."

Jane dug her heels in Lightning's flanks and headed down the street at a gallop, jumbled emotions coursing through her, and a lump in her throat. Riding fast felt best, just now, feeling how the pony responded to her, how the pony knew her and anticipated her moves. The speed fed her anger at first; and then she realized it. Lo had given her the pony BECAUSE the pony knew her best. With Lo gone, the pony knew her better than her friends did, better than her family did, and Lo had known that she needed that. She slowed down to a stop. The lump faded.

Mr. Fergus and Andrew were ahead, outside the Fergus home. She headed in that direction. Mr. Fergus seemed stern, Andrew glum. Jane reined in her pony and gracefully hopped off before her steed had even come to a complete stop.

"Good morning, Jane," said Mr. Fergus. "You're in fine spirits this morning."

"Ain't every day a girl gets a new horse," she said.

"Looks like your old horse," said Andrew.

"Yeah, but now he's my horse," said Jane.

"Oh," said Andrew.

Mr. Fergus gave Andrew a pat on the back and a nod. "You two have fun, but don't you be late again, Andrew." He headed towards town.

"You catch hell for being late for school?" Jane asked.

"Yeah."

Jane thought she knew what would cheer him up. "You wanna ride my pony?" she said, beaming.

"No, Goddammit, I don't want to ride your fricking pony," Andrew growled.

Jane was sure knocked back on her heels by this. Andrew almost swore at her!

"You got a great deal here," said Andrew. "You're Calamity Jane. You don't have to go to school every day. You play cards all day while they bring you coffee and pastries. Me, I gotta go to school so my Dad doesn't have an illiterate for a son." With that, he wheeled around and headed towards school, leaving Jane with her pony's halter limp in her hand.

Jane felt that old ache in her stomach rise to her throat as she watched Andrew walk further and further away. She hadn't felt that ache since the first night they met. When she saw that he wasn't going to turn around to wave goodbye, she swung up on her pony. "Let's go, Lightning," she said.

They zigzagged through the jumble of sluices at the edge of the creek, drawing quizzical gazes from miners as their cheerful greetings went unanswered. Jane pressed Lightning for speed on the trail out of town. She wasn't headed far, though. As in Bannack, in Alder Glick lived just on the edge of town. Jane covered the distance at a full gallop. She had never ridden Lightning at this speed before, and the exhilaration eased her mind.

As soon as she hopped off Lightning, she heard a familiar yelp and the padding of paws. Lucky came to greet her with all the energy of a puppy, though now he was nearly full-grown.

"Hey, boy," she said as she scratched behind his ears. "How's my favorite dog?"

Glick's door was closed. Jane knocked.

"Who's there?" Glick called.

"Calamity," was her reply.

"Come in, m'darling," said Glick.

Jane pushed the door open. In the dark cabin she could see two figures besides Glick, and a scene that reminded her of her stint as a nurse. Surgical instrument in hand, Glick was bent over her friend Mr. Ezekial. As her eyes adjusted, she was relieved to see that Glick was working on nothing more vital than his foot. The third person in the room was Dez.

Glick cut the tension in the air by breaking into song, barely looking up from his work.

Oh, m'darling,
Oh, m'darling,
Oh, m'darling C'lamity!
You are lost and gone forever, dreadful sorry, C'lamity.

Glick clanked the side of a bucket with his forceps after every time he sang "C'lamity."

"I'm sure you know my patient, Calamity," said Glick.

"Morning, Calamity," said Mr. Ezekial.

"I imagine you know my nurse, too." Glick nodded to Dez.

Jane felt a tinge of jealousy when he used the term "my nurse." She was supposed to be his favorite nurse. "Dez," said Jane.

Glick continued his song.

"By the river lived a maiden,
In a cottage seven by nine,
And around this lovely bower,
Blessed sunflower blossoms twine.
Oh, m'darling,
Oh, m'darling,
Oh, m'darling C'lamity!
(clank)
You are lost and gone forever, dreadful sorry, C'lamity."
(clank)

"That ought to do it," said Glick.

"I'm lucky it wasn't worse," said Ezekial.

"What happened?" Jane asked.

Ezekial took a big sigh. "A man with whom I had never before had the pleasure of acquaintance came into my store this morning. He decided for some reason that he deserved a number of items for free. I was foolish enough to argue the point, so he took out his Bowie knife and threatened to, as he put it, turn me inside out."

"How awful," said Dez. "Why didn't you pull your gun on him?"

"Might have had to use it, then," Ezekial replied. "And I better shoot him dead, or he would come after me for sure later. And then, if I shot him dead, well, then there would be a trial. And the outcome of a trial around here depends as much on your popularity as it does your guilt or innocence."

"So what did you do?" Jane asked.

"I tried to be clever. I told him he could pay me back later."

"By the looks of your foot, he didn't go for that," said Jane.

"He looked like he was considering it for a moment, but yes, the result is obvious," said Ezekial.

"Were you scared?" asked Dez.

"Sure was, facing the business end of his gun. He squinted down the barrel at me for a moment, then kind of snarled and shot my foot instead."

"Could have ended much worse for you, Ben," said Glick.

"This is terrible," said Dez. "What are you going to do?"

"There's not much to be done," Ezekial said, shrugging.

"Goodness," said Dez. "Crime is like the weather around here. Everybody talks about it but nobody does anything about it. Why not go to the Sheriff?"

"Getting killed is the only way to get the law involved around here, I'm afraid," said Ezekial. "Anything short of that and it's considered a private matter between myself and the gunman."

"Well, I don't care what you say," said Dez. "I'm going to have a talk with the Sheriff as soon as we are done here."

"Feel free," said Ezekial. "Word is, he's in Skinner's."

Dez hesitated. "Jane will come with me. She's not afraid of anything. Won't you come with me, Jane?"

"Sure," said Jane. The best protection available for a foray into Skinner's was to travel in the company of the prettiest girl in town, and she wanted to observe the man she now suspected to be the worst of the worst. "Come on, Dez," she said.

So Dez removed her apron and washed her hands. Then she and Jane headed for town, leading Lightning toward the stables first. "Skinner's, huh?" said Dez.

"That's what they said."

"There's an Indian scalp nailed up over the bar."

"You seen it?" asked Jane.

"No, are you kidding?" said Dez. "I've never been in that place. Have you?"

"Nope."

"It's probably okay now, if the Sheriff is in there," said Dez.

"They will leave us alone. Anybody shoot you, that would be the end of him," said Jane.

"Right," said Dez. "All I have to do is bat my eyes to get what I want."

Jane had largely lost all consciousness of her tomboy garb, except when she was around Dez. She wondered what it would be like to be a beautiful woman.

"I hear this miner killed hisself 'cuz you wouldn't pay him no mind," said Jane.

"Yeah." Dez frowned. "There's a lot of lonely men in this town, but you can't imagine how that hurt me."

"I s'pose," said Jane. "Anyhow, you should do the talking when we get there. All eyes will be on you anyway. I'll read them for what they ain't telling us." They were at the stables now and Jane gave Lightning to the stable hand.

"You good at that?" Dez asked.

"Good at what?"

"Reading men."

"You learn that around a card table," said Jane.

"That's something," said Dez. "This ought to be fun."

So with their plan in mind, the girls proceeded to Skinner's and pushed through the door, past the multipaned windows, and into the lair of the local lowlifes.

A hush fell over the saloon. About the time that Jane's eyes had adjusted to the darkness, the silence was broken by a solitary voice, with an emphatic, "Goddamn!"

"Hold on there, boys," came a voice, "I think we can all refrain from profanity for as long as these divine feminine creatures wish to grace us with their presence." It was Plummer.

"For the one, anyhow," came a voice. Again, silence.

Jane looked around. There was tension on the faces of the men, a look like they had seen a lot of violence, and were ready for more once "these divine feminine creatures" had departed.

"Sheriff, we need to speak to you," said Dez.

"It would be my pleasure," said Plummer.

"I'd like to give her a good talking-to," came a voice from a corner. Men laughed, but were silenced by a look from Plummer. Interesting, thought Jane. Plummer exerted authority here. She searched for familiar faces and found Greaseball.

"How may I help you, my dear Dez?" said Plummer.

"We are here," said Dez, "because our friend, and pillar of this community, Ben Ezekial was shot today."

Snickers rose from another corner. Plummer rose and strode in the direction of the snickering. "You men know something of that?" he asked.

There was an unfamiliar face at a card table in that corner. He laid a card on the table. "I heard of it," he said. "Storekeep couldn't dance fast enough, I hear tell."

"You know who shot him?" asked Plummer.

"If I did, what of it?" said the man. "It was just his foot."

"Seems like you might have been pretty close to the action," said Plummer.

"Word travels fast is all," said the stranger. "Like I said, it was just his foot. He can take it up with the feller that shot him any time he wants, if he has a mind to."

"You are new in Alder, so this is a good time for me to tell you that I don't like that sort of thing in my town."

"I'll tell that to the feller what told me about it," said the man. "Maybe it will get back to the one that done it."

"There's women and children in this town," said Plummer. "Maybe it isn't like the last place you got chased out of."

"I'll be sure to pass the word along," he said.

"Ben Ezekial knows who he was anyhow," said Jane. "Why don't you go ask him, Sheriff?"

Again quiet descended. Jane's gaze was drawn to the scalp nailed over the bar.

"That's right, Sheriff," said the stranger. "Why don't you go do that?"

"I think maybe I will," said Plummer.

"You don't sound very serious about this, Sheriff," said Dez. "What if Mr. Ezekial had been killed?"

"But he wasn't, was he?" said Plummer. "If your Mr. Ezekial had been shot dead, I would hunt the shooter down, and then there would be a trial. That's my job. Short of that, it's considered a matter between the two men. You two run along now," he said to the girls. "I'll be sure to talk to Mr. Ezekial."

Dez gave Jane a look, then tossed her head towards the door. They slowly stepped outside, but once in the street broke into a run.

"Come on," said Jane, and she led the older girl to the edge of the stream of muddy water that ran through the center of Alder Gulch, surrounded by the constant earthmoving activities of the miners. Panting, the girls looked at each other wide-eyed. "Did you see the scalp?" asked Jane.

"Ew, it was disgusting," said Dez. "I never saw a place like that before and I hope I never see one again. What do you think Plummer is going to do?"

"Don't know," said Jane. "Seemed awful familiar with them boys."

"That fellow at the card table didn't seem to be scared of him," said Dez.

"Took it all as a joke," Jane agreed. "Dez, can you keep a secret?"

"Sure," said the older girl.

"I got my suspicions about Plummer," Jane said. "Lo and I was robbed on the trail once, and I'm pretty sure of who one of the boys is that done it. And then I seen that feller with Plummer, acting like old chums. So I got to thinking. When they robbed us, they said they had a boss. What if Plummer is their boss?" Jane didn't want to tell stories about Glick, so she didn't add that Glick had spoken to those men of their boss that night they worked on Lefty's arm.

"My goodness!" said Dez. "You have such an imagination! The Sheriff? Are you saying he's a bandit? My word."

"Don't know, just speculation," Jane said. "Someone is the leader, and I just got a feeling."

"That's crazy talk," said Dez. "But I tell you, somebody has got to stand up to the outlaws. Look at all these miners," she said, waving towards the mass of men working the banks of the creek. "They all just want to get rich and get out of here. They aren't going to risk their necks to bring law and order to this place. But to me, this is my home."

"I like it here," said Jane. "I ain't going back to Missouri."

"I like it here, too," said Dez. "Somebody has to make the place fit for the likes of us."

Chapter 12

Autumn passed, and winter fixed its icy grip on Alder Gulch. The miners could no longer make their claims yield gold, as water would have frozen in their sluices, so they relied on their savings from the warmer months—at least those who had been wise enough to save anything. A storekeeper, or a man who worked in a sawmill like Bob Canary, could still ply his trade, but the need for his goods and services was diminished. With more time on the men's hands, the prostitutes and dance hall girls still did a brisk business, though their prices came down some. For her part, Jane dealt Faro and bantered with the men around the table. She thought of Lo sometimes as she pulled cards from the silver box he had taught her to use, and hoped he was well on his way to San Francisco.

Boredom came to dominate Alder. For the better class of men like Mr. Fergus, reading was a favorite pastime to combat the tedium, but reading material was very scarce and highly sought after. Newspapers arrived in Alder months after the events they chronicled, but they were so precious that they were read and reread for months after that. Now, in early winter, the most recent newspaper was four months old and had been worn to a flimsy collection of shreds by the great many who read it over and over. The few books in circulation were read aloud over and over again to attentive audiences, no matter what the subject matter. The wives of Alder were not immune to the boredom. Mrs. Vail, who ran the only boardinghouse in town, started a Wednesday Bible study, which was well-attended by the good women of town. Dez attended these meetings and attracted a clutch of men who tried to act like they were attending for their spiritual edification. The other women saw through their artifice, but none complained, for they were hopeful that religious services would awaken in these men a civility which the community as a whole sorely needed.

For the lower class of men, boredom, lubricated by drink, gave rise to fighting. The spark that inflamed their passions so was often the war back in the States. In July, around the time of the stampede to Alder, the Southern city of Vicksburg fell to Northern forces, and that same month the Battle of Gettysburg ended in the North's favor. The news of these battles travelled quickly about the nation by the singing wires of the telegraph, reaching Salt Lake City by that amazing form of modernity. From there, cryptic versions of the news reached Alder at the speed of plodding oxen, but full details had only recently arrived by the New York newspaper. With winter in force now, newcomers to the goldfields slowed to a trickle, and the net effect of this combined with flaring tempers in the saloons was that the burial ground overlooking town now grew faster than the town itself.

Late one November day, Jane sidled into Kustar's bakery after work. She loved the smell of fresh bread in the bakery, and better yet, the pies! As she fingered her day's pay, she imagined Lana's eyes lighting up at the sight of such a treat, and the two of them sharing these sugar coated delights.

The proprietor of this bakery was aware, as Lo had been, that the best way to make money in a mining town was to sell whiskey. Kustar's bakery for this reason had a bar staffed by a burly bartender, and there were tables where a man could wile away the tedium with a game of cards.

As Jane waited her turn at the counter, she took note of an argument that had broken out in a game of euchre. Insults were being tossed at the dealer regarding his honesty, his intelligence, and the marital status of his mother at the time of his birth. This fellow was a reasonable sort, and did not particularly take offence at the picture thus painted of his honesty or his mental capacity, but he did draw the line at being called a bastard. Jane's ear was attuned to such exchanges by her experience at the Faro tables, and she felt that this would likely settle down. She ordered her items from Mr. Kustar, and noted that Greaseball was slinking in a corner, looking haggard and hungry, and casting furtive looks at the baked goods so close at hand. Greaseball had fallen on hard times, it seemed, and become one of the "bummers" who hung around waiting for a handout.

Suddenly, the dealer of the euchre game took the verbal offensive against one of his detractors, and rose to his feet to make his point more explicit. Jane surmised that it was now in her best interest to put some distance between herself and this scene, but unfortunately, the game table was between her and the door. Euchre is a game of partners against partners, so naturally the argument divided two against two across the table. The players soon fell on each other with fists. The dealer came to the conclusion, however, that fisticuffs would not sufficiently redress the insults he had endured. He drew a Bowie knife, as did his partner, but in an escalation that they had not anticipated, pistols were drawn by their opponents. Jane ducked under the counter, and watched with dreadful fascination, conscious that Greaseball crouched just behind her. She figured that this coward just intended to use her as a shield, but she misapprehended his intention. Mr. Kustar and his bartender raced behind the gun-wielding combatants in order to restrain them, but in doing so, they only managed to shift the advantage to the men with knives, who attacked with vigor. The restrained men still managed to get off several thunderous gunshots that lit the room with flashes of light, and filled it with the acrid smell of spent gunpowder.

The gunshots hit the log walls harmlessly, though one knocked a big dough paddle off its hook. Jane would have paid this no mind and kept her eyes on the action, but the paddle struck her and came to rest awkwardly on her legs. She turned to push it away so it would not trip her in case the opportunity arose to make her exit. As she did, she saw Greaseball place a berry pie on the floor. This puzzled her, but more shots called her attention forward again. The dealer lunged at the gunman who had earlier shown such disrespect for his mother, and dealt a Bowie knife to his thigh. The injured man dropped his gun and fell to his knees, cursing loudly, his thigh bleeding onto the dirt floor. Kustar and his bartender had by this time managed to disarm the other gunman, so now they were able to tackle the dealer and put an end to the melee. The exhausted gladiators yielded to Mr. Kustar's loud epithets, and put their weapons away. The wounded man's friends offered to help him to Dr. Glick's, which he refused. He did allow them instead to each take him by a shoulder and help him hobble away from the scene, leaving a trail of blood behind.

Jane scowled at Greaseball for his cowardice and he sneered back. The bartender and baker started to clean up the mess from the melee.

"You boys done yourself proud," Greaseball said to them. Indicating Jane, he said, "Coulda been someone hurt."

Jane knew Greaseball wouldn't have shed a tear if she had been shot dead, but Kustar acknowledged this observation with an appreciative grunt.

"Here, let me help y'all clean up," said Greaseball, as he tipped chairs upright and tidied up. He picked up the dough paddle and hung it back on its hook, then pointed to the pie Jane had seen him place on the floor and another just like it, their tops smashed. "Oh, ain't it a shame," he said.

The baker leaned over to see. "Oh, well," he said. "If that's the worst of it, we got off light." He bent over to pick them up, saying, "I'll throw them out."

"No need for that," said Greaseball. "I'd pay a quarter apiece." The undamaged price was a dollar apiece.

The baker was about to agree to the bargain, but Jane spoke before he could. "Damn shame, those ruined pies," she said. "Strange, though, how they didn't bust apart when they fell on the floor. And that dent in the crust—looks like a knuckle print to me." The baker looked at Greaseball suspiciously, and then at his hand, which Greaseball furtively moved out of sight.

"It's a fair offer," he hissed.

"Could be," said the baker. "Calamity is such a good customer, though, I think I'll make a present of these to her." He scowled at Greaseball as he gave the pies to Jane. Jane took the pies carefully, one in each hand, and proceeded towards the door. Greaseball growled like a beaten dog, and lunged toward her, his face in hers, close enough so only she could hear him whisper, "Too bad about your friend."

"I got lots of friends," Jane said, shrugging. She was not afraid of Greaseball, but he was so close now that she could feel his hot breath, and it turned her stomach sour with its mix of rotten teeth and wasted whiskey.

"The yeller one what taught you Faro, missy, that one. Too bad," he said.

Jane glared at him.

"Such a tragedy." Greaseball eyed her intently and made a strangling motion to his neck, then repeated it with a gurgling sound, his eyes half-closed.

Jane heaved a pie at the vile little man's face while he still had his eyes half-closed. "Take your pie then, jerk-off. You're talking about my friend."

The others turned from their clean-up. Greaseball pulled a fragment of the pie off his cheek, and ate it with a vengeful scowl. "Waste of good pie," he said to the room. "Well anyhow, I tried to help, no matter what y'all think. Guess I'll be on my way." With a smirk, he brushed the rest of the pie onto the floor and sauntered out of the bakery.

Jane followed him to the door and shouted after him. "You're just lucky I been learnt to act like a lady, asshole!"

Chapter 13

The cold days of isolation and boredom wore on. Back in the States, President Lincoln declared the first Thanksgiving holiday, and word reached Alder just in time to celebrate the new holiday, at least in the homes of Northern sympathizers. Emissaries of President Lincoln arrived with news that the gold rich area had drawn the attention of government, and the area was to be organized into a territory of the United States. Sheriff Plummer hosted a Thanksgiving banquet for this group, which included an energetic lawyer named Sanders. The Ferguses attended this banquet, and later Andrew regaled Jane with a description of the magnificent feast the Sheriff provided.

After that, Alder settled into a winter tedium. The male population drank and played cards, fought and made up, spun yarns, played pranks on one another, and found female companionship in a dance hall or in the arms of a prostitute. Supply trains still occasionally made the grueling trip from Salt Lake City, now and then breaking Alder's collective boredom and maintaining a tenuous thread of contact with the outside world. Every day that Jane dealt Faro at Madam Chi's, she felt Lo's absence, and she tried as hard as she could to put out of mind what Greaseball had told her. His words tormented her, and she strained to convince herself that he was just trying to rattle her. Even when she was able to convince herself that Lo must be okay, she still wished that she had warned him that she suspected Plummer was the chief bandit, that he should secret all his activities from the man.

She kept all this to herself, even though it ate at her insides. She didn't tell Chi, as her words could only hurt. She didn't know who to trust and she didn't know who would listen, so she confided in no one.

One night, asleep with her family and wrapped snugly in her buffalo hide, Jane had a dream. She was riding Lightning on a snow-covered mountain when a quail flew into view. She pulled out her rifle and bagged the bird. When she went to retrieve it, drifts of snow impeded her progress: first knee-high, then chest-high. Somehow she finally reached the quail, but when she reached for it, it became a frozen hand poking out of the snow. The scene shifted. Lo appeared to her, smiling a bigger smile than he ever had in real life. He showed Jane his new dance hall in San Francisco, teeming with gamblers and dancers, dancing and gambling away to the most happy music. Then the music turned to a low, ominous rumbling. Jane awoke with a start, breathing heavily and sticky with sweat. It was pitch black, and everyone else in the family was fast asleep. She stared at the wall until she managed to get back to sleep by listening to the music of Lana's peaceful, deep, easy breathing.

The next morning, Jane ate a quick breakfast in silence. A cloud of gloom clung to her thoughts.

"Something wrong, Jane?" asked Ma.

"Naw. Just had a bad dream," Jane replied. She sopped up bacon drippings with a chunk of bread, tossed on her heavy overcoat, and parted company with her family. Slamming the door behind her, she took the well-worn path towards town, past idle sluices and frozen mounds of gravel. She stopped to look at the snow-capped mountains, cold and forbidding in the distance. Crossing the bridge to town, she headed to Ezekial's store, not wanting to start her day at Madam Chi's just yet. Mr. Ezekial was in good spirits this day, engaged in an animated discussion with Dez as he limped behind his counter.

"Morning Dez, morning Mr. Ezekial," said Jane.

"Good morning, my darling C'lamity," said Ben Ezekial.

"If you start singing, I'll be forced to take my business elsewhere," said Jane in jest.

"Then silence is golden, my dear," he said. "What can I do for you today?"

"Nuttin', just looking for company," said Jane. "Had a bad dream last night."

"Bad whiskey will do that," said Dez.

"I don't drink whiskey," said Jane. "It's against my religion."

"And what religion might that be?" asked Mr. Ezekial.

"I'm a agnostic," said Jane. "That means I don't know what the hell to believe."

"I'll thank you to not swear in my establishment, Calamity," said Ezekial. "Especially in the presence of a lady."

"Who, Dez here?" Jane screwed up her face. "She's heard worse or else she ain't paying no attention at all."

"Tell us about your dream," Dez said.

"Had a dream that Lo's been killed," said Jane. The smiles dropped from her friends' faces. "Anyhow, thing is, I got the feeling from this dream I'm s'posed to do something."

"Like what?" said Dez.

"I don't know what," said Jane. "What could I do?"

Mr. Ezekial looked at her pensively. "I believe dreams can have great portent and meaning. What did the dream mean to you?"

"His arm. The one with the tattoo," said Jane. "I saw his all-seeing eye tattoo on his arm."

"Interesting," said Ezekial. "That's a Masonic symbol."

"Yeah, Lo was real proud of being a Mason," Jane said.

Dez heard it first and held her finger up to silence the other two. A low rumbling in the distance. "Supply wagons!" she said. "Come on, Jane, let's go see if they brought any perfume, or hats, or licorice!"

That rumbling. Jane dragged her feet as she followed her friend, a sense of foreboding stifling any urge to hurry. The wagon train was fording Alder Creek and the first of its number was making its way up the hill. She recognized the driver of the lead wagon as the same

Mormon whose partner had been killed in Bannack. Dez slowed when she saw his grim visage, but Jane ran ahead, anguish in her heart.

The driver tried to stop her. "This is not a sight for young eyes, my child," he said, holding up his hands.

These words only confirmed Jane's worst fears. She ran to the back of the still-moving wagon and followed silently. Dez caught up and took Jane's hand, trudging along with her friend. Word spread quickly, and men poured out of the stores and saloons and followed the wagon uphill. Madam Chi came to her doorway to assess the commotion, and when she saw Jane's gaze fixed on the wagon's cargo, she hurried to her protégé's side. There, partially covered with blankets, was a frozen body. Jane gave Chi a hug.

The driver stepped down from the wagon box and walked to the rear of his wagon. He stopped facing Madam Chi. "I do not know you, madam, but you may be able to identify one of your own kind."

Chi came closer as the driver beckoned, her chin raised to steady a quiver. The driver lifted a blanket enough for her to see the body.

"Lo!" she cried out, as if the wind had been knocked out of her. She fell to her knees, and Jane leaned down to steady her and comfort her in her grief.

The driver climbed on the back of his wagon so all in the growing crowd could see him. "My name is Palmer," he said, in a booming voice. "Yesterday, on the trail, hidden from sight, we found this body. There are things here all should see."

Jane helped a tearful Madam Chi to her feet. Someone had summoned Dr. Glick, who pushed his way to the front of the crowd. Jane could see Mr. Fergus coming forward as well, and her Pa approached the outskirts of the crowd.

Mr. Palmer lifted the blanket off Lo's body, then addressed the crowd. "Look. Rope burns around his neck. And this. Drag marks all over his body. He was dragged through the brush by a rope around his neck. And look. Look at his frozen hands. What do you see? Balled up in his fists. What do you see?" Palmer stepped back for all who wished to see.

Silently men filed past, grim-faced. Jane could not bear to look and hugged Madam Chi, steadying her trembling form.

Palmer called out to the crowd, "In death he still grasps sage in his fists. The Chinaman was alive when he was dragged through the sage, pulled by a lariat around his neck."

Swarthy miners stood with callused hands hanging limp and self-conscious at their sides. Shock deadened the faces of Fairweather and Edgar, normally so carefree and celebratory. Other men, the denizens of Skinner's saloon, who spent all their time at drink and cards, stood with cocked heads and nonchalant manner, as if to say that they had seen this sort of thing before.

Palmer continued, "Imagine, all of you, how he grabbed the sage desperately as he fought for his life. And here. A bullet hole above his eye. That ended his misery."

Palmer turned to Glick for confirmation.

"What he says is true. See for yourself, any who want to," said Glick.

Palmer had the gift of a voice that projected to the last man at the edge of the crowd without shouting, a deep bass voice that reverberated in a man's chest like a bass drum. "My partner was shot a few months ago by such men as did this. His crime in their eyes was to fire at them in self-defense. What could this Chinaman have done to deserve a fate worse than that?" Palmer paused. The crowd was silent. "Nothing," he thundered. "I tell you that there is nothing that he could have done that would have made this a deserved end to his life."

Muttering arose in the crowd. Among the miners, there was an upswelling of outrage, and more than once Jane heard "enough is enough." But the saloon denizens mocked the miners and flung racial slurs at Lo and Chi. Jane felt herself flush, and she saw Madam Chi stiffen at the word "chink" tossed around among these men.

"Out of the way, Sheriff coming through." Plummer pushed his way to the wagon. He examined the body. "This here is an outrage. There's many a man met the same fate on the trails 'round here and every one is a tragedy." He turned toward the men from Skinner's and said,

"Anyone says different just because this boy is a Chinaman has to answer to me."

"I say, enough is enough!" said Mr. Fergus. "Sheriff, we should round up men to ride out and find those who did this."

Several outraged voices in the crowd volunteered.

"What do you say, Sheriff?" said Mr. Fergus. "Will you lead us?"

"All right," said Plummer quietly. "Let's go find the men who did this."

"That chink left here near a month ago," Greaseball called out. "You ain't gonna find no trail with these tenderfeet."

"John Innis can track anybody anywhere," said Fergus. "Will you ride with us, John?"

"I'm your man," Innis said, with as much confidence in his manner as there was economy in his words.

"Goddammit, let's string the scumbags up!" shouted one of the volunteers, and there rose up a chorus in agreement.

"Now hold on," said Plummer, "I've said it before and I'll say it again—I won't be part of any lynching. If I am to risk my neck on this wild venture, it's to bring the accused back to a jury trial. Here. In Alder. We will be a territory of the United States of America soon. And let's keep the language down—there are women here."

The crowd's mood shifted. Their outrage over this heinous act was supplanted by a sense of helplessness. Men who had shouted in anger now shuffled their feet and mumbled about the futility of a trial, and some turned away.

The silence was broken by Madam Chi, who let out a loud wail and pushed between Glick and Plummer. She seized Lo's frozen hand and brought her cheek to it, all the while wailing in Chinese. Jane tugged her gently, then firmly, and pulled her away. As she turned away, the last thing she saw was Lo's tattoo and its all-seeing eye, his proud badge of courage.

Ezekial climbed up on the wagon to address the dispersing crowd. "This man was a Mason. I will hold Masonic rites for him tonight out at the burial grounds. Anyone who wants to pay proper respects is welcome.

Chapter 14

Pa had let a beard grow over the last few months, as many men did in Alder, shaving being a bit of a nuisance on the edge of the wilderness. But now was a time to show respect. Even the Indians looked at a beard as unbecoming, referring to full-bearded white men as "dog-butts," so the beard had to go. Pa borrowed a mirror from a neighbor and carefully shaved with a straight-edge razor as Lana watched in fascination. He then dressed in a white shirt he hadn't worn since he had sat at poker tables in Bannack. Ma offered Jane her own best dress to wear, but the only time Lo had seen her in female attire had been the first day they met, so she decided to say good-bye dressed as he knew her.

Jane was to be an honored guest at the Masonic rite, as was Madam Chi. Poor Lo. Sorrow filled Jane's heart, but more than that, agony. The thought that she might have been able to save him tortured Jane more than ever, but at least Lo was going to get honored as a Mason, and she knew that would have meant a lot to him.

Pa had been asked to escort Jane and Madam Chi to the burial grounds. Jane and Pa walked silently on the path Jane had taken so many times to Chi's saloon. When they arrived, Pa lit a torch and knocked. The torch threw off dense smoke, and lit Madam Chi's face with flickering light when she came to meet their summons. She looked regal, wearing a stiff blue silk dress with a Bengal tiger emblazoned on it, which seemed to dance in the torchlight.

"Ma'am," was all Pa said as he nodded to Chi.

She returned the gesture with a deep bow. "You honor Madam Chi and Mr. Lo. Thank you, sir," she said. Jane took Chi's hand, and Chi grasped her tightly as they followed Pa in the eerie torchlight.

The burial grounds were on a small knoll, which gave the deceased a view of Alder in its entirety. The silky moonlight glossed over the grimy details of the town, and it looked downright picturesque from this vantage point. Ben Ezekial stood in front of Lo's coffin, while Mr. Palmer provided light for this somber scene with his torch. Palmer and Ezekial wore aprons with gilded symbols upon them, the all-seeing eye at the apex. A gaping hole in the ground with fresh-dug earth piled beside it awaited the conclusion of the ceremony. Andrew and his parents, Dr. Glick and a few others stood at a respectful distance from the grave. Andrew gave Jane a comforting nod as they joined that group.

Ezekial stepped forward and bowed to Chi. "

"Allow me to honor brother Lo with this," he said. He untied his apron and placed it on Lo's coffin.

It seemed to Jane that the all-seeing eye on the apron examined them all.

"Brother Ezekial, would you please commence services?" Mr. Palmer asked.

"It would be my honor," said Ezekial. "Good citizens of Alder, we gather this evening to bid farewell to a good man, who, unknown to myself and Palmer was a fellow adherent of the Order of Free and Accepted Masons."

Palmer signaled Ezekial to stop and pointed in the direction of town. Approaching uphill was another torch, and as it came closer, Jane could see that it was carried by the German fellow who had raced Plummer's horse, with friends.

"Charles Beehrer, Stuttgart, Germany, Chapter Seven, Free and Accepted Masons," he said somberly on arrival. His friends introduced themselves one by one as well, and named their respective Masonic chapters in Germany.

"Willkommen, mein Deutschenbrüder," said Ezekial. Jane felt Madam Chi's grip on her hand tighten as the Germans bowed to Chi. The Deutschenbrüder gathered in a semicircle facing their deceased fellow Mason. Ezekial cleared his throat and opened the Bible from which he was to read. When he looked up, though, he paused and squinted. Jane could see a look of surprise on his face, and she turned toward town where he gazed. A dozen or more torches were making their way towards the service, bouncing gently as with measured tread each group came to pay their final respects.

Cecil was the first of that number to arrive, with his torch lighting his large apron. "Brother Cecil Jones, African Lodge number 1, Boston," he said in his deep baritone voice. Mr. Ezekial did not hesitate to call out, "Welcome, Brother Cecil."

The preacher who had competed with the peddler for souls that day of the horse race introduced himself and named his chapter. More torch-bearing groups arrived; miners, calloused hands holding torches aloft; a tinsmith, and a frail-looking newspaperman newly arrived from England. One by one they gave their names and the names of Masonic chapters either back in the States, or, for the younger men, chapters in places like Rough and Ready, California, and Virginia City, Nevada.

Madam Chi seemed to rise above her natural height, standing more proud and erect with each new arrival. She squeezed Jane's hand, transmitting her pride and bringing a lump to Jane's throat.

A particularly intense man introduced himself, "Wilbur Sanders, men, personal envoy of President Lincoln." Finally the train of torches ended. The semicircle around Lo's coffin shifted and adjusted into double rings, then triple. A frigid breeze fluttered the apron that lay on Lo's coffin. Tears welled in Chi's eyes, but she made no sound.

Mr. Ezekial projected his voice to the gathered Masons. "Brothers, I hope you all feel the same warmth I feel at being able to call other men brothers at this perilous time. All of us see each other as we pass on the street, and we tip our hat sometimes and nod, but we did not know each other as brothers until now. I am as guilty as any of letting suspicion separate me from the good men gathered here: suspicion borne of ignorance, and accentuated by the politics of a distant war. We come here to honor a man who lived among us, and who most of us thought of as a stranger. He should not have been a stranger to us, for he was as much a part of the fabric of this remote community as you or I. That he was not friend to any of us is not itself a shame, perhaps, but his fate is certainly a shame—if not to each of us individually, then collectively. Let us come together now, that others do not suffer a similar fate as that of Brother Lo, my brother whom I barely knew."

The breeze blew fine snow about the feet of Lo's mourners. Ezekial continued, "I will now read a verse from that part of the Bible which is common to all our religions." He nodded to Palmer, who returned the gesture. Ezekial began:

"The hand of the Lord was upon me, and carried me out in the Spirit of the Lord, and set me down in the midst of the valley which was full of bones.

And caused me to pass by them round about; and, behold, there were very many in the open valley; and, lo, they were very dry.

And he said unto me, 'Son of man, can these bones live?' And I answered, 'O Lord God, thou knowest.'

Again he said unto me, 'Prophesy upon these bones, and say unto them, 'O ye dry bones, hear the word of the Lord.'

Thus said the Lord God unto these bones: 'Behold, I will cause breath to enter into you, and ye shall live.

And I will lay sinews upon you, and will bring up flesh on you, and cover you with skin, and put breath in you, and ye shall live; and ye shall know that I am the Lord.'

So I prophesied as I was commanded: and as I prophesied, there was a noise, and, behold a shaking, and the bones came together, bone to his bone.

And when I beheld, lo, the sinews and the flesh came upon them, and the skin covered them above: but there was no breath in them.

Then said He unto me, 'Prophesy unto the wind; prophesy, son of man, and say to the wind, 'Thus saith the Lord God: Come from the four winds, O breath, and breathe upon the slain, that they may live.'

So I prophesied as he commanded me, and the breath came into them, and they lived, and stood upon their feet, an exceeding great army."

A much colder wind blew now than the one in that ancient passage, but it found embers to fan in the hearts of men.

When Jane awoke the next morning, she saw a white crust on her buffalo robe. Ma was up, starting a fire in the stove, while Pa and Lana still slept.

"There's a hole in the roof," Jane said, thinking snow had fallen on her bedding.

"No, girl, that's frost from your own breath. It's cold enough outside to freeze the tail off a brass monkey, and only a little warmer in here. I'm working at getting a fire going."

Jane decided to wait until it warmed up a little before she would venture from her warm buffalo robe to dress. It felt luxurious to huddle in the warmth of her bed.

"You girls are so lucky," said Ma, as she fussed with the stove. Oh, God, thought Jane, here it comes again. The "you girls are so lucky" talk.

"When I was a kid, we didn't have no sheet-iron stove that kept the heat through half the night," Ma said.

Great, thought Jane. So as a result, I have to listen to you complain about it forever.

"I grew up in a log cabin, just like this one, 'ceptin' we had a wooden chimney, plastered inside," Ma continued.

"And every night..." Jane mentally continued Ma's story.

"And every night, we had to bank the fire so's there would still be coals the next morning," Ma said.

"And if the chimney caught fire," Jane continued the story out loud, rolling her eyes.

"Oh, so maybe I did tell you this a time or two before," said Ma. "Well, won't hurt you none to hear it again. If'n the chimney caught fire, we was s'posed to knock out a particular log halfway up the chimney, so's to collapse it and the whole cabin wouldn't go up in flames."

"Musta been something, livin' back then," Jane said, her voice dripping with sarcasm.

"You don't know how good you got it," Ma continued. "Warn't no such thing as no kerosene back then, neither, and no telegraph. And I would have given my eye teeth to have been able to toddle down the street to see all the excitement you got here, what with violin players and all manner of carousing, and my Lord, every Sunday is like the circus come to town. All's I'm sayin' is, you should count your blessings sometimes, Missy. You ain't got such a bad life."

Jane put up a bratty façade, but she was comforted by the familiarity of this exchange with Ma.

Lana stirred. "Look," she said. "I can see my breath."

"I'll take Queenie out after breakfast," Jane said.

"Where you going to go?" asked Ma.

"Andrew's." Jane had a feeling something might be afoot, the way the men had acted after Lo's funeral.

"Don't go outside," Lana admonished Jane, "'cause then you could get frostbite."

Jane lay down by Lana and wrapped a hide around the two of them. "You know I ain't one who could sit inside all day, no matter how cold it is. Let me cuddle you to keep us both warm for a time."

"Do you miss Mr. Lo?" asked Lana.

"Sure do. But it's weird. I'm mad at him, too."

"How come?" asked Lana.

"'Cause he left without saying good-bye, I guess."

"Don't be mad at him," said Lana. "He's dead now."

"I s'pose I shouldn't be," said Jane. She couldn't tell her sister that on top of all that, she felt an aching guilt because she had kept a secret that might have somehow saved him. She changed the subject. "I wish your doll hadn't fallen apart, 'cause we could play with it together now."

"I don't need dolls no more," said Lana. "I want to come with you and deal cards."

"You do, huh?" Jane teased. "Wouldn't you be a sight. Hafta sit on a crate to be tall enough to reach the table."

"Would not. I'm big enough."

Well, you might be big enough to learn to hunt this summer, did you know that?"

"Really?" Lana said. "Ma can I learn to hunt this summer?"

"That's your Pa's business," said Ma. "Ask him when he wakes up." Jane gave Lana one more hug. "So for now, you keep Ma company, and I'll be back soon." Jane hopped out of bed, dressed in every stitch of clothing she owned while standing as close to the stove as she could get.

"Breakfast will be soon," said Ma.

"I'm not so hungry," said Jane. "I'll grab something at the bakery." It was nice to have a little money. She called Queenie, then said goodbye to Ma and Lana.

The still air hung over an unusually quiet town. Jane only saw a couple of men on the streets hurrying in straight lines from one place to another. The chill stung her face, and her boots crunched the frozen ground. Faint strains of a lone violin intermittently penetrated the still air. Jane stopped for a moment to see how large a cloud of frozen breath she could blow, then continued on her way. As she walked up the hill toward town, she heard a lumbering wagon. There they were. Coldest day of the year, but Robert and James were hauling firewood. "Hey, boys," she called as they got closer.

"Hey, Calamity," James piped. Robert nodded sourly.

"You boys trying to keep warm by swinging an axe all day?" she said.

"This is when folks need firewood the most," said Robert.

"You're the business man," said Jane. "You see anything unusual this morning?"

"There's a lot of horses missing from the stables," said Robert. "You know something about that?"

"Nope," she said.

"Sorry 'bout your friend," said James.

Jane nodded. "He was a prince. Anyhow, see you 'round."

Robert slapped the reins on his horse and the wagon lumbered away.

"Let's go talk to Andrew, Queenie. See what he knows."

Queenie whined as they turned up the path to the Fergus' home.

"What's the matter, girl?"

Queenie barked towards closer homes.

"Too far in this cold, eh, girl? All right, then let's go see what Dez knows. She knows everybody. Might have heard a rumor flitting about."

Dez's mother came to the door when Jane knocked.

"What can I do for you, my dear?" she said. Her manner was aloof and businesslike. Jane was still the daughter of a fallen woman to the married women of town, reformed or not, and that Jane dealt Faro all day long didn't help in their eyes.

"I'm looking for Dez," Jane said.

"Well, then," said Dez's mom, "Don't stand there with the door open and heat the whole outdoors. Come in."

Church lady, thought Jane. Queenie curled up in a ball outside the door, and Jane entered the warm cabin.

Dez rose from her breakfast. "Bye, Mom," she said as she pulled on a long coat. "I think I'll go to Kustar's bakery. Bring us back some pies if everything in town isn't frozen solid."

As she whizzed out the door, Dez grabbed Jane's hand and pulled her along. "Come on," she said.

Queenie barked a greeting.

"Oh, Queenie, my favorite pooch." Dez scratched and patted her. "I wish I had a fur coat like yours." She turned to Jane. "Sorry about Lo. Are you okay?"

"Yeah," Jane said. They proceeded to the bakery, with Queenie following.

"I've been watching Plummer since you told me about him and his friends," said Dez after a bit.

"I just got a feeling," said Jane.

"He disappears for days, and then when he comes back he looks like something the cat dragged in," said Dez. "Makes me wonder. Where should we go after the bakery?"

"I was headed to Andrew's. You heard anything?"

"About what?"

"The Fitzpatrick boys say there's a lot of horses missing from the stable."

"Haven't heard anything, but I haven't left the house 'til now," Dez said, shrugging.

The warmth of the bakery felt glorious and the aroma of fresh-baked bread was intoxicating.

"Morning, Dez," said one of the men, rising eagerly to his feet from his card game. One after another of the card players called their greetings to the town's sweetheart.

"Hey, Calamity," called one as an afterthought. The attention showered on Dez gave Jane a twinge of jealousy. After all, it hadn't been that long ago that her presence here hadn't even given pause to a brawl.

"What's news today, Mr. Kustar?" Dez asked.

"Just danged cold is all," Kustar replied.

"Allow me the honor of buying you a pastry, my dear Desdemona," said the swain who had greeted her first.

"Aw, he can't afford to buy you much the way he's been playing today, Dez," rang in one of the others. "Let me buy you a pie."

"You bought her one last time," said a third man. "It's my turn."

"Goodness, gentlemen," Dez said, with a graceful gesture towards Jane. "I would like to honor the generosity of each and every one of you, but I have only two hands." The smarter of her swains took the hint and bought Jane a pie while the others bought two for Dez, and in return they all received a nod and a coo from the object of their affection. Dez leaned close to Jane. "Let's get out of here," she said.

Dez turned down offers to carry the pies, and the girls swept out of the bakery, three tasty pies between the two of them. The men called after them, telling them to stay warm and return at their first opportunity, and Queenie chased along behind the girls.

Dez giggled. "They're sweet."

"Where did you get the nickname 'Dez' anyhow?" Jane asked.

"Oh, one of my boyfriends is a real reader. He started calling me that after a character named Desdemona in Shakespeare, and it stuck. I kinda like it."

"Who's your favorite?" asked Jane.

"Favorite boyfriend? I don't know," said Dez lightly. "I like a man with a lot of self-confidence, in a relaxed kind of way. Most of these boys have a sort of desperate air about them, when they are around me anyhow." She paused and sized up Jane. "Do you have a boyfriend?" she asked.

"Naw," said Jane.

"How about Andrew? Is he your boyfriend?"

"He's just a friend," said Jane. "We kind of had a falling out anyhow."

"Oh, then," said Dez, "why are we bringing pies to your boyfriend's house?" She handed one of her

two pies to Jane so that she only carried one and Jane had two.

"He's not my boyfriend," Jane protested.

"Your booooyfriend!" the older girl said, and she turned towards the Fergus house. "I'm going to knock on their door and ask if Calamity's boyfriend is home!" She laughed and ran ahead.

"Stop—he's not. My. Boyfriend!" Jane panted, as she struggled to run after the older girl, awkward as she was with a pie in each hand. But Dez was at the Fergus' door, pounding furiously and laughing as hard as she could. Jane arrived at the door and butt-checked Dez, laughing hard herself.

The door swung open, and a dour-faced Mr. Fergus appeared. The girls tried to stop laughing, but trying to be serious only made them laugh harder.

"Can I help you girls?" asked Mr. Fergus.

"We brought Mrs. Fergus a pie," said Dez through her giggles. "Here. Can Andrew come with us?"

Mr. Fergus took the pie and stepped back to reveal Andrew, holding a slate, sitting on a three-legged stool as his Mom stood over him with a book. "Aren't you a little old to be playing with my boy?" Mrs. Fergus asked Dez.

"Well, Jane wants to have a word with her boy-friend." There was a hiccup between "boy" and "friend" as that word passed Dez' lips, induced by a sharp poke of Jane's elbow to her tormenter's ribcage. "And I'm here to chaperone." She stomped on Jane's foot. Jane screwed up her face in pain and stifled a high-pitched cry.

"I'm not too worried about these two needing a chaperone, leastwise in this weather," Mrs. Fergus said with veiled condescension.

Andrew rose from the stool, eager for any chance to escape his lesson. "Where we goin'?" he asked.

Minutes later, the trio was on their way, blowing small clouds of frozen breath between bites of shared boysenberry pie, with Queenie trotting happily behind. There was a half-built building on Main Street that they knew they could have to themselves, so they headed there. Inside the doorless building, Jane contemplated the solid beams of the unfinished ceiling above them. I bet Pa cut those beams, she thought. They piled some wooden boxes on top of each other and draped a tarp over that for shelter. After arranging it all to their satisfaction, they sat and ate their pie.

"Sorry about Lo," Andrew said.

"He didn't deserve what he got nohow," said Jane.

"Something is up," said Dez to Andrew. "You hear anything today?"

"Didn't have visitors before you and it was too cold to go out."

"Fitzpatrick boys say a lot of horses are missing from the stables," said Jane. "Gotta be a good reason to go out in this cold. I bet the Masons have gone after Lo's killers."

"Jane thinks Plummer is the leader of the bandits," Dez explained to Andrew.

"The Sheriff?" said Andrew. "Are you crazy?"

"It ain't so crazy," said Jane.

"I don't know if he is or isn't," said Dez, "but he goes missing for days with no explanation."

"You two are crazy," said Andrew. "He's the Sheriff."

"Well," said Jane, "somebody is chief of the bandits around here." She recounted the whole story of the wounded bandit and the bullet that couldn't be found.

"And Glick asked them where their boss was, 'cuz he threatened to kill him before," said Jane.

"Who threatened to kill him?" asked Andrew.

"The boss. The time before."

"So why is that the Sheriff?" he asked.

"'Cuz I seen the Sheriff with this guy that I know robbed us, acting all chummy," said Jane.

"Robbed who?" asked Andrew.

"Me and Lo."

"You're crazy."

"I ain't crazy."

"What do you think the Masons will do if they find the killers?" Andrew asked.

"Probably they'd string them up where they find them," said Dez.

"Could be a gunfight," said Jane.

"Probably one or the other," said Andrew.

Queenie, who had been keeping their feet warm, whimpered and thumped her tail. The conversation turned to the cold weather, then to other bad weather they had endured; each trying to top the stories of the others about tornadoes back home, or lightning that caused buffalo stampedes on the way to Bannack, and so forth. They concluded that they were the veterans of the goldfields now compared to all the tenderfeet that had streamed into Alder in the past few months. Finally they became talked out, and parted with an agreement to watch for developments and to notify each other as soon as there were any.

Chapter 15

At breakfast the next morning, distant shouts floated to the Canary cabin from the direction of town. Jane jumped to the door and peered out.

"They're back," she said.

"Who's back?" asked Ma.

"The Masons."

"Get dressed and see," said Pa.

Jane jumped into her second and third layers of clothes and hurried out the door.

It was a grim group of Masons that sauntered back into town. They were twenty slouching, haggard men surrounding three prisoners on horseback: Weasel-Snout, Glass-Eye, and Lefty. John Innis trailed, leading Lo's mule, Black Bess.

Evidently, word had been sent ahead by the group, because a crowd was already gathering in front of the unfinished building in which the trio of pie-eating friends had conjectured the day before. Miners and merchants put down their work and headed to town center, and riff-raff sauntered from the saloons. Two wagons had been set next to each other, in one of which Mr. Fergus conferred with the lawyer, Smith, and Sanders, Lincoln's envoy.

Jane ran up to Mr. Ezekial, who leaned down to her, face weathered, his frostbit hands barely grasping the reins of his horse.

"We got 'em," he said.

"I know them boys," said Jane, indicating the prisoners, as they were placed up on the second wagon.

"Glick told us," said Ezekial. "Not sure how this is all going to work out. There's more of the gang somewheres about. And you know about Plummer."

Jane scanned the crowd for a moment. "Watch out for that one." She indicated Greaseball, who was flitting back and forth, nervously craning his neck to see what was going on.

"I'll let the men know," Ezekial said. "See Lo's mule?" He tossed his head in that direction.

"Sure."

"She's key evidence. You might need to testify that it's his. Was his anyhow," said Ezekial.

"Sure," said Jane.

Mr. Fergus called from one of the wagon boxes. "Spread the word—miner's meeting in thirty minutes."

Thirty minutes looked to be plenty. If there had been a telegraph set in every home, saloon, store, shop, dance hall, and brothel, word of the trial could not have traveled more quickly. Hordes of men streamed to Main Street from all directions. Some of the miners took it upon themselves to build fires for warmth near the wagon. The Kirkpatrick boys had stored cords of wood nearby, and the brothers looked on helplessly as men appropriated the fruits of their labor to warm themselves. Skinner and other saloon keepers brought out their plank bars, but armed Masons grimly put a stop to that.

Jane saw Andrew and Dez climbing up on the windowsill of the unfinished building. She weaved her way through the gathering crowd. "Hey, Andrew, Dez."

"Hey, Calamity," they said in unison.

"I guess we were wrong about the lynching," said Andrew.

"And about the gunfight," said Jane.

"You think these are the boys that killed Lo?" asked Dez.

"They had his mule," said Jane. "Anyhow, them are the ones that shot the Mormon."

"Come on up here," said Dez. "We have the best seats in town."

"Can't," said Jane proudly. "I might have to testify."

"Wow," said Dez. "Aren't you scared?"

"Time for that is passed," said Jane.

"I don't see Plummer," said Andrew. "Where's he?"

"Dunno," said Jane, "but I should go." She left her friends and headed back to the wagons, pushing through a crowd now numbering several hundred, and growing by the minute. Men breathed clouds of frozen breath in the air as they stomped their feet, clapped their hands together, or jumped up and down a little—anything to keep warm. As many as could fit surrounded the fires built from the Kirkpatrick boys' firewood.

All was prepared now—in a makeshift kind of way. The prisoners had been placed under guard of Jane's friend, the gentle giant Cecil. Each had different reactions to their predicament. Lefty was angry and sullen, while Weasel-Snout was nervous and fidgety. Glass-Eye looked morose and contrite as much as he looked confused.

Mr. Fergus finished his conversation with Sanders and Smith. He climbed onto the wagon box with a rifle borrowed from the German, Beehrer, and fired it in the air. The crowd quieted.

"Miner's court in session," shouted Mr. Fergus. "The prisoners you see before you stand accused of the murder of the saloon keeper, Lo. Mr. Sanders will serve as prosecuting attorney. Smith here is counsel for the defense. Mr. Sanders, please proceed."

"This ain't right," shouted Greaseball. "Murder case oughta be a jury trial!"

"What, so's you can point a gun at the jury?" came a voice from the crowd.

An uproar came from those who supported a jury trial, most vociferously from the saloon denizens, and there was some support from fair-minded men as well.

"All right, then," said Fergus. "I will entertain that motion. All in favor of a jury trial, say 'aye.'"

There were loud ayes from Greaseball and his ilk.

"All opposed, say 'nay,' " Fergus continued.

The nays were not as loud individually, but there were many more of them, and their voices rumbled in the cold air.

"Motion failed," said Fergus. "Mr. Sanders, proceed."

Sanders looked like a man to be reckoned with. Proud and self-assured, he looked like he was scouting the crowd, weighing the mood and temperament of them all. "I first call to witness Mr. Palmer."

Palmer climbed the wagon. "Mr. Palmer," said Sanders, "describe for us how you found the body of the saloon keeper Lo."

"Many here know me and will know that I am an honest man not prone to tell tales," said Palmer. "Three days ago on the trail, I was walking in front of my team, rifle at the ready for bandits. I saw a quail take flight, and as a reflex I took a shot at it. I'm a poor shot, and I don't think I could hit it again even if I was loaded with birdshot. The Almighty guided the bullet, though, and it struck my target. The bird fell, out of sight of the trail. I halted the others in my wagon train while I went to retrieve my quarry. I found the bird lying on the chest of the dead man, in a clump of heavy sage brush, completely concealed and away from the road, where no one would have gone except by chance. I might not have even seen it from ten feet away the way the body was hidden in the snow and brush. I can think nothing other than that Divine Providence led me to this man's body."

"Crazy Mormon," called out Greaseball. "How many wives you got back home?"

"Did you see any indication of the killers nearby?" asked Sanders.

"I could see their campfire over the crest of the next hill," he replied.

"Objection!" called out Smith. "This man, overwrought as he is with the religious fervor so common to those of the Mormon cult, is jumping to the conclusion that the nearest campfire was that of the killers. We all know Lo had been missing for weeks. Saying that this campfire in the general vicinity of where the body was found was that of the killers is the sort of convenience resorted to by a lazy mind."

"So noted," said Fergus. "Miner's court will weigh your objection as each man individually would see fit. Please continue, Mr. Sanders."

If looks could kill, Palmer's glance would have at least maimed Smith.

Sanders called his next witness. "Mr. Innis, I understand you are a competent tracker. Would you say

this to be true?"

"I would," replied Innis. "I have tracked man and beast for days and weeks at a time."

"Were there signs that led from where the body was found to the hideout of these men?"

"Objection, your honor," said Smith. "Calling the dwelling of my clients a 'hideout' implies they were hiding, which they were not."

"All right," said Fergus. "Please reword that, Mr. Sanders."

"Were there signs," repeated Sanders, "that led from the murdered man's body to the shelter where you found these prisoners?"

"There was the most obvious path of broken sage and hoofprints, as if the man had been dragged by a horse from the trail to the spot where we found him," said Innis.

"That is all, your honor," said Sanders.

"Your witness, Smith," said Fergus.

"Mr. Innis," said Smith, "you say the path was from the deceased man to the trail, correct?"

"That is correct," said Innis. "In the direction of the hideout."

"Shelter, you mean," said Smith. "But the signs you followed led to the trail, correct?"

"Yessir."

"Where did the trail lead from there?"

"Well, dozens of men travel that trail every day," said Innis. "Any signs are wiped out by all that traffic, of course."

"Of course," said Smith. "Did you try to pick up the trail again somewhere closer to the shelter in which you found my clients?"

"Sure."

"But I take it you did not find such a trail, right?" said Smith.

"That's right," said Innis.

"How far from the shelter were you when the drag path ended at the trail?"

"A couple hundred yards."

"A couple hundred yards?" asked Smith. "And dozens of men on the trail would have encountered Lo on the trail and have had opportunity to rob him. Absurd. I have no further questions at this time, your honor."

"Seems a bit close to be just coincidence," called out Fairweather.

"They're innocent!" shouted Greaseball, to a chorus of agreement from his sort. Fergus called for order. "Next witness, Mr. Sanders," he said.

"I call Ben Ezekial," Sanders called out. Ezekial climbed onto the wagon. "Describe for all of us,

us," said Sanders, "the arrest of these men."

"We waited some hours in the dark and cold for the first rays of light," said Ezekial. "Then, with guns drawn, we all entered the shelter while they were still asleep."

"And what did you say to them?" Sanders asked.

"I said that they were all under arrest for murder, and that it would go hard on anyone who didn't cooperate."

"What did you do next?" Sanders asked.

"We took this man aside for questioning," said Ezekial, indicating Glass-Eye.

"Sir, what is your name?" Sanders asked Glass-Eye.

"I ain't no sir, but my name is John Franck," Glass-Eye mumbled.

"John Franck. How did you lose that eye?"

"Brother threw a rock at me when I was a kid."

"Did you have trouble with figures and numbers after that?" asked Sanders.

"Objection," cried Smith.

"What?" said Fergus.

"I do not see how my client's childhood bears on the unfortunate demise of the saloon owner Lo."

"Judge," said Sanders, "I intend to show that Mr. Franck does not have the mental capacity to lead these men and show why we picked him to question."

"Proceed," said Fergus.

"Did you have trouble with figures and numbers after that injury?" asked Sanders.

"Hard to say. Not much call for that where I growed up," said Glass-Eye. "They said I was out for a week after that, though, and I had fits ever since."

"I see," said Sanders. "Mr. Ezekial, please resume your story, and tell us of your questioning of Mr. Franck."

"So myself, Mr. Palmer, and John Innis took Mr. Franck here to where the body had been found while the others of our party kept watch over the other two."

"What was your purpose in that?" asked Sanders.

"We intended to trip him up in a lie, if possible, or, after getting his testimony, trip up the next man we questioned," said Ezekial.

"So you brought him to the site where the body had been found," Sanders continued. "What did you say to him?"

"I told him that this was where Palmer had found the body, showed him how a trail led towards where he lived, and asked what he knew about it."

"And what was his response?"

"At first he said he didn't know anything about it, but just then, a black mule came wandering towards us."

"What mule is that?"

"The one over there tethered to the wagon," said Ezekial.

"Continue, Mr. Ezekial."

"So, I asked him, 'whose mule is that?', expecting him to name one of the other men in the hideout."

"Objection, your honor," said Smith. "Could you please instruct the witness to strike the term 'hideout' from his lexicon?"

Mr. Fergus raised his eyebrows. "Can you do that, Mr. Ezekial?"

"My apologies, Judge," said Ezekial.

"Continue, Mr. Sanders," said Fergus.

"So a black mule came within sight, and you asked the prisoner whose it was," Sanders said. "What did he say?"

"Well," continued Ezekial, "he said, 'That is the mule that the Chinaman rode here.' Just like that."

"And what do you find so significant about that?" Sanders asked.

"Up to that point, we had not told him who had been murdered," said Ezekial. "He incriminated himself that simply."

The crowd rumbled angrily, as tempers flared among those outraged by the murder. But Greaseball countered that sentiment. "I don't believe a word coming out the mouth of that storekeep. Jewish asshole just wants to make money on the rope it would take to hang poor John Franck!"

Scattered laughter came from Greaseball's friends.

"Silence!" Fergus shouted. "There is nothing about any of this to joke about. This is a murder trial. A man is dead, the victim of an outrageous act of treachery. You here, all of you, will decide the fate of the court's prisoners. Every man brings his prejudices to this trial. It is the duty of every man present to set those prejudices aside. If you can't set those prejudices aside, you are hereby commanded to keep your mouth shut. And if you cannot keep your mouth shut, I will have you forcibly removed."

Greaseball slunk to another part of the crowd.

Fergus continued, emboldened by the favorable crowd reaction to his speech. "Mr. Sanders, please proceed."

"Mr. Franck, will you please confirm to everyone that this is Mr. Lo's mule?"

"Yeah, that's it," said Franck.

Jane was disappointed. Looked like she wouldn't have to testify on behalf of Lo.

"Was there anything Mr. Ezekial just said about you and the mule that was not accurate?"

"No," said Franck.

"Judge, may we confer with you and Mr. Smith for a moment?" said Sanders.

Fergus addressed the crowd. "Miner's court in five minute recess. You men stand at ease."

Crowd noise swelled as the men argued the situation among themselves. Numerous voices called for Franck to hang. Sanders, Fergus, and Smith moved together to talk privately. Sanders and Smith argued, eventually coming to an agreement.

"Thank you, Judge," Sanders said. "Now, Mr. Franck, I am prepared to put your guilt to a vote. Are

you ready for that?"

"What the hell choice do I have?"

"What if I were to offer you a choice?" said Sanders. "I know that you were at least a witness to this murder, but you are not the sort who would have led anyone in this despicable act. The men who did this to Lo deserve to hang. But I am willing to see that instead of hanging, you are only banished, if you will tell us what you know."

Glass-Eye cast a furtive glance at Greaseball. "I may be stupid, but I ain't crazy. Banishing don't do me no good, even if you do hang these two."

Sanders persisted. "Everyone here can see that you were likely just a bystander in this murder. Please. Just tell us what happened."

Glass-Eye looked Sanders in the eye. "I can't do it," he said. "If you don't get the chief, you might as well hang me now."

"Who is the chief, Mr. Franck?" asked Sanders, loudly for the crowd. "Say it, and I will see that he is put on trial."

"You can't touch him," said Glass-Eye.

"He is under arrest right now. I can bring him forward now or at any time that suits us," said Sanders.

That surprised Glass-Eye. "And I get banished if I testify?"

"We are willing to do that, despite your crimes," said Sanders. Fergus nodded.

Glass-Eye paused with his head down as he thought, but after a while he shook his head. "Half the folk here wouldn't believe Secesh like me if'n I said the sky was blue," he said.

"Tell us who the leader is, Mr. Franck," said Sanders. "Tell the crowd. You will be banished if you testify, but if not, we will put your guilt to a vote."

Glass-Eye paused again. Slowly, he shook his head. "I have to take my chances."

"Very well," said Sanders. "Judge, I would like to set aside the case against Franck for the moment and proceed with another case."

Fergus looked to Smith, who offered no disagreement. Glass-Eye was moved to the other wagon and replaced with Lefty, who grimaced in pain as he was moved.

"Please state your name for the record," said Sanders.

"John Wagner."

"Mr. Wagner, you stand accused of the murder of the Mormon..." He turned to Palmer, who provided the name.

"Now hold on a minute, Judge," said Smith. "This is the murder trial of the Chinaman Lo. What is this amateur prosecutor doing now?"

"Judge," Sanders responded, "these three men and others like them have been terrorizing this area for over a year. Every honest man here knows that when he travels on the surrounding trails, he takes his life in his hands. This trial is not only about Lo, but about every man within the sound of my voice."

"How do you plead?" Fergus asked Lefty.

"I am innocent!" shouted Lefty.

"Your Honor, I respectfully request to confer with my client," said Smith.

"Certainly."

"Don't need that," said Lefty. "You can keep your slick ways to yourself, Smith." He faced the crowd with a look of defiance and shouted again, "I am innocent!"

Jane was surprised at the audacity of Lefty's assertion, and the convincing manner with which he said it.

"Present your case, Mr. Sanders," said Fergus.

"Gentlemen of the miner's court, I call William Palmer to the witness stand again."

Palmer climbed up to the wagon box. He faced the crowd, resolute and imbued with righteous fervor.

"Mr. Palmer, please relate to everyone here how your partner was killed in July of this year."

"We were a few hours' ride out from Bannack on the last day of our trip from Salt Lake City," said Palmer. "My wagon was attacked by three masked bandits, firing guns in the air. I was driving the team, and my partner was riding alongside me, rifle at the ready. Brave man that he was, my partner shot and wounded one of the bandits as they approached. In return, the villains riddled him with bullets. I stopped the wagon and surrendered."

"In what manner was the bandit wounded?" asked Sanders.

"He was shot in the inside of his right elbow," said Palmer.

"Thank you, Mr. Palmer," Sanders said. "I now call Dr. Glick to the witness stand."

Glick climbed up on the wagon box.

"Doctor Glick," said Sanders, "On the day in question, did you treat a man with a gunshot wound to the elbow?"

"Yes," said Glick.

"Is that man here?"

"He is. Mr. Wagner here."

"He's lying," said Lefty. "I'm innocent."

"Please tell us the circumstances, Dr. Glick," said Sanders.

Glick hesitated and searched the crowd. He looked one notch better than timid right now, and Jane was afraid he would be unpersuasive. Jane took heart from Sanders, though, standing fearless before the crowd, leading by his wits. "I can tell that story, Mr. Sanders," she said.

"Dr. Glick?" asked Sanders.

"Miss Canary was present at the time. As you may know, I am a well-known Southern sympathizer hereabouts, and I think my testimony would be discounted by many. If Miss Canary is willing to testify, she can just as well inform you as could I."

"Very well," said Sanders. "Miss Canary, will you please take the stand?"

Jane felt a wave of excitement as Glick helped her up on the wagon.

"You can do it," Glick said.

Turning around, she faced a sea of faces, a thousand men, every gaze locked on her.

"Miss Canary," said Sanders, "Were you at Dr. Glick's home on that day?"

"Yes sir, we had just finished eating."

"Thank you for your willingness to bear witness. Please tell us all what happened."

"Well, these other two," she indicated Weasel-Snout and Glass-Eye, "brought in Lefty here."

"By 'Lefty', do you mean Mr. Wagner?"

"Yes, sir."

"Are you sure this is the man?" asked Sanders

"Well, he was breathing down my neck for a couple of hours while Dr. Glick poked around in his arm for the bullet. We became pretty familiar, the three of us."

"So you were close enough to see the wound?" asked Sanders.

"I was Dr. Glick's nurse while he worked on it," said Jane. "If I had been any closer I would have fallen in." Jane was beginning to relax.

"I am innocent!" Lefty again asserted.

"Tell us then, Mr. Wagner," said Fergus, "your version of the events."

"I don't know nothing about no robbery," said Lefty. "I got this wound when I slept too close to a campfire. My clothes caught fire, and the bullet fired from the heat."

"I see. Let us test whether that could be true," said Sanders. He took a bullet out of his own gun and found a stick in the Fitzpatrick boys' woodpile, and cut a notch in it with his knife. "I will wedge this bullet on this stick and place it in the fire."

"Your Honor," Smith said to Fergus, "I really must protest. This in no way replicates what Mr. Wagner is describing."

"Shut up, Smith," said Lefty. "I told you I don't want no help from you."

"Mr. Smith," said Fergus, "I'm sure the court will take your concerns into account anyway."

Sanders proceeded to the closest fire, and the men who had been warming themselves around it parted. "I have tied a handkerchief around the bullet to replicate clothing the accused would have worn and I have placed it very close to the flames," he said to the crowd. "Mr. Fairweather, please come closer as a witness for those who cannot see from where they are. Please describe to them what is happening."

"The cloth is steaming or smoking, can't tell which," said Fairweather.

"When the cloth burns, call that out to the crowd," said Sanders.

There was a pause of less than a minute. "Cloth's burning," said Fairweather.

"And still the bullet has not fired," said Sanders. "How long will it take, do you think?"

"Count of twenty, I'm guessing," said Fairweather.

"Five will get you twenty it takes a minute!" called out a voice from the crowd. There was scattered laughter.

"Again I remind you men," shouted Fergus. "This is a murder trial. A man was killed in a savage manner and those responsible deserve to die. Behave accordingly, or go find entertainment in a saloon."

"The cloth is all burned off now," said Fairweather.

With a bang, the bullet fired. Sanders held the stick aloft for all to see. "Mr. Wagner, you would have been burned to a crisp before your gun would have fired."

"He's innocent!" shouted Greaseball. "Your powder was wet."

"I would be glad to repeat this process with any bullet you might supply," Sanders replied.

The crowd seemed divided in their opinions. "He's innocent, he said," Greaseball called out again. "This is an illegal trial! Where is the Sheriff?"

"All in due time," said Fergus. "Mr. Sanders, please continue."

Sanders climbed back up on the wagon. "So, Miss Canary, you were within inches of the wounded man for a long time, is that correct?"

"Yep," said Jane.

"Can you describe the man's wound to us?"

"Well, his arm was swole up about double normal size. There was a hole at the inside of his elbow where the bullet went in, but no bullet hole going out, so obviously the bullet was still in there somewheres."

"Mr. Wagner, will you please show the court your arm?"

"I don't have to show nobody my arm," said Wagner, twisting away. He backed into Cecil, who grasped his shoulders. Lefty gasped in pain. "Never mind, nigger," Wagner said. "Y'all can look. Don't prove nothing. I was wounded when I slept too close to the campfire."

Cecil released Wagner, and held Lefty's coat while the prisoner gingerly pulled his arm out of the sleeve, and then pulled up his shirt-sleeve.

"Mr. Fairweather, will you examine the prisoner's elbow and describe that to the rest?" said Sanders.

"Be quick about it," Wagner said. "It's damned cold, in case you hadn't noticed."

Fairweather climbed up on the wagon and peered at Lefty's elbow from all angles. "One bullet hole on the inside of the elbow. Only that one."

"So men," Sanders addressed the crowd, "Mr. Palmer describes that the bandit had a wound very much like this one, and Miss Canary says that she and Dr. Glick attended to this man's wounds on the evening of the robbery. I don't see how any reasonable man could doubt that Mr Wagner robbed Mr. Palmer."

"The girl is lying," Greaseball called out. "How come she didn't tell anyone if what she says is true?"

"Well, they threatened to kill Dr. Glick and me if we told," Jane answered.

"Yes," said Sanders. "Who made that threat?"

"This other feller," said Jane, indicating Weasel-Snout.

"She's lying!" said Weasel-Snout. "You can't believe a whore's daughter."

"I am not a liar!" Jane shouted. My Ma was a whore, but she ain't now, and she don't raise no liars." Jane scanned the faces in the crowd, a thousand men focused on her alone. "My Pa was a drunkard gambler, but he ain't no more, and even when he was, he was no liar either." She met eyes with one man after another as she spoke. "Dozens of men been killed on the trails around here. This here trial is about two of them, and one of them was my friend. He was a Chinaman, and the other feller was a Mormon. Maybe you're from some faraway place I ain't never heard of and ain't never going to see, and you think these men been killed ain't the same as you. And prob'ly you plan to make your pile of gold and get out of here as fast as you can. So you wake up every morning and you think that this place is a hellhole that you don't have to treat no better than you treat a whore. But this is my home. Me and my friends, the kids whose wood you burn right now to keep warm, the little girls who pick your greens so's you don't get the scurvy, the girl you got a crush on, this here is our home. Ain't none of us going back to the States, I'm telling you, with all them soft folk with no sense of adventure. Now's your chance to clean this place up and make it fit for us. And fit for you, if you got the gumption to stay."

The crowd fell silent. Jane looked to her friends across the way. The first voice to break the silence came from an unexpected quarter. "You tell 'em, Calamity!" shouted Robert Kirkpatrick.

"Hang the bastards!" shouted one of the miners. A roar of agreement went up from the assemblage, and there was a surge towards the wagons. Fergus raised his arms and shouted for calm, to little effect. Fairweather stepped up on the wagon, calmly borrowed a rifle from a Mason, and fired it in the air twice. The crowd settled down. Fairweather gave the rifle back to the Mason and stepped down.

"Thank you, Mr. Fairweather," Fergus said. "We will now put the question of how to proceed to a vote."

Mr. Fergus took voice votes as to whether to hear more evidence and which prisoner's guilt to put to a vote first. It was voted to try Lefty first, since the greatest weight of evidence was against him. A few upstanding men in the crowd felt that the trial had not been to the highest standards of fairness, and when the vote was taken, those few voted against conviction, along with Greaseball and his friends, but the overwhelming vote was for conviction. During the vote, Ben Ezekial sent Cecil to his store on an errand, and when the big man returned with a length of rope, he fastened it to a timber which was then itself fastened like a flagpole to the outside of the unfinished building. Jane watched in dreadful fascination as these preparations were made right under the noses of Dez and Andrew. Wagner, still sullen and defiant, was prodded to this makeshift scaffold by Cecil and Ben Ezekial. They contrived an unsteady tower of boxes, placed the noose around his neck, and hoisted him up on the boxes.

"Have you anything to say before you meet your maker?" Fergus asked the doomed man.

"Damn right I do. You are hanging the wrong man."

"Mr. Wagner," said Fergus, "there has been a fair airing of the evidence, and it is the determination of this court that you are guilty."

"Well," said the condemned man, "at least you are hanging the wrong man first."

"That could be," said Sanders.

"There's one I want to see hang before me, so's I know he gets his, too," Lefty snarled.

"Perhaps that can be arranged," said Sanders, "should you wish to tell your story."

"Could take some time. I can't balance up here so good tied up like this. If you want to hear what I have to say you better untie me," Lefty said. "Otherwise I could slip and y'all will never know what I have to say."

Sanders and Fergus agreed to this request. Cecil was directed to untie the prisoner's left arm, which he stretched out and brought to his neck.

"Stop right there," said Fergus. "The rope stays."

"Suit yourself," said Lefty. "I just want to remove my tie. Do you think you boys could see your way to bringing me a tall glass of Tanglefoot?"

"Good God, man! What sort wants to meet his maker drunk?" asked Fergus.

"I don't 'spect the devil is going to care if I'm drunk," said Lefty.

Fergus sent a man to fetch the drink.

Lefty slowly removed his thin black necktie with his good hand. It dangled in his fingers for a moment while he considered what to do with it. His eyes met Jane's. "Remember what I told you about choosing your friends," he said, and tossed the tie to her. "That was a damn fine speech you made. No hard feelings." He guzzled the whiskey when it was brought to him and tossed the tumbler to Glick carelessly. "If I'm lucky I'll be half drunk by the time you boys kick out my perch here. Now, seems to me you got some questions for me."

Sanders took a breath. "I have it on good authority that this was not the first time one of your fellow bandits had been brought to Dr. Glick for a gunshot wound. Is that correct?"

"No, there was another time."

"And on that occasion, a prominent citizen accompanied you, correct?" asked Sanders.

"Now you're talking," said Wagner.

"This man was your leader, correct?" said Sanders.

"Yep. He told Dr. Glick that himself."

"Why do you think Dr. Glick did not come forward with that information?" asked Fergus.

"Could be because this here prominent citizen threatened to kill him," said Lefty.

"Do you mean that maybe Glick was threatened, or that the threat caused him to hold his tongue?" asked Sanders.

"What do you think?" asked Lefty. "The boss told Glick point blank that if word ever got out about any of this that he would personally kill him."

"Tell us all who that man was," said Sanders, "and more directly, who is the leader of the band of outlaws who has terrorized this area for the last year?"

Lefty scanned the faces of the men who would watch his last minutes on Earth. "Henry Plummer," he said.

"Bring up the prisoner!" Fergus shouted, before the crowd exploded in disbelief. A guard of two men had been waiting nearby for the command, and brought a struggling Plummer through the back door of the vacant building.

Fergus waited for the crowd to settle down. "Henry Plummer, you stand accused of leading a gang of men that has murdered dozens of good men these past months. How do you plead?"

"This is all absurd. Innocent, of course," said Plummer. "As your Sheriff, I demand that you, Judge Fergus, put a stop to this illegal proceeding immediately. And take this man down from there. I will allow no lynching while I am Sheriff!"

Crowd reaction was split. Some were incredulous that Plummer could be the leader of the gang, others angry that he was. Greaseball, however, decided he was not taking any chances, and furtively headed for the stables. He did not notice that the German Mason Beehrer followed him.

"Plummer, you have the right to face your accuser," said Fergus. "Dr. Glick, tell your story."

"Mr. Plummer," said Glick, "one evening in the spring of last year, you brought a man to my cabin for treatment of a gunshot wound. He had received this injury in the course of committing a robbery. I tended to his wound to the best of my ability, but he died, and you told me that if I ever told of that affair, you would kill me."

"I don't know anything about this," Plummer protested. "You Secesh trash, I can only guess your motives for making up such a story."

"So you deny that you are the leader of a band of robbers and murderers that has plagued this area for many months?" asked Sanders.

"How could anyone here even consider such a possibility?" asked Plummer.

"'Cause I told them so," said Lefty. "That's exactly who you are. The leader of a band of twenty-odd assholes like me, who were drawn together by your smooth manner. Or your threats, like poor John Franck here."

"Your response, Mr. Plummer?" asked Fergus.

"I am innocent of all of this trumped-up nonsense," said Plummer. "All you men know me. I am the Sheriff! I have been diligent in all my duties and an upstanding citizen at all times. I had no involvement in these heinous crimes, and no association with this profane man. I appeal to the sense of decency of you men of this jury—for all of you assembled are my jury—do not be swayed by the drunken ravings of a condemned man with a noose around his neck, and a Secesh doctor who has always had it in for me."

The crowd murmured as it contemplated Plummer's words. Up until minutes ago, few among them had suspected him of much worse than arrogance.

"I say he's guilty!" shouted Fairweather, and the same was voiced over and over in the crowd. Mr. Fergus held up his arms for quiet. "Those in favor of a guilty verdict for Henry Plummer, say 'aye.' "

The "ayes" were deafening.

"Those opposed, say 'nay.' "

There were a few nay votes, but they were scattered and anemic.

Cecil threw another rope over a beam inside the building, and tied a noose in it.

Plummer called to Fergus as these preparations were being made. "Your Honor, if your eyes are blinded to the injustice of this, I beg you, at least banish me. I swear, I am innocent."

"Justice has been served, Sheriff," said Fergus as the noose was placed around the condemned lawman's neck. Cecil and Ezekial lifted him onto boxes under the beam.

"Judge, spare these children the spectacle of seeing me hanged," said Plummer. "Banish me, brand me, cut off my ears, but spare my life."

"I don't see what these children would gain by watching us cut off your ears," said Fergus. "I think they benefit more by knowing you are dead."

"Cut off his ears like he wants," said Edgar. "Then hang him. He was supposed to be the law." There was a sprinkling of grim laughter.

"Your time has come, Sheriff," said Fergus. "Do you have any last wishes?" Plummer faced Lefty,

mirror images, each on his own gallows. Lefty sneered at his boss, who straightened up and surveyed the crowd.

"I wish for a mountain to jump off, but if you boys will promise to give me a good drop, suppose this will do," said Plummer.

Fergus nodded to Cecil and Ben Ezekial. "Men, do your duty."

The two fellow Masons crouched down, and on the count of three knocked the boxes from under Plummer's feet. The crowd was absolutely silent; the only sound heard was the creak of the rope as it wore a slight groove in the beam over which it had been slung.

Lefty broke the silence. "Kick away, Chief. I'll be chasing you through hell soon enough."

Beehrer returned, with Greaseball as his quarry.

"Yeah, he's one of us," said Lefty, and he named the rest of the gang of thieves and murderers that had plagued the area, and detailed the robberies they had committed. When he had finished, Cecil and Ezekial positioned themselves on both sides of Lefty's precarious pedestal. When Lefty was given the opportunity of last words, he turned his face to the sky and shouted, "Hurrah for Dixie!" and jumped before the men could move.

Attention turned to Weasel-Snout, who trembled and stammered some details of the men named by Lefty, along with their misdeeds, hoping that by doing so he could win banishment. His efforts, however, were to no avail, and soon his limp form was swinging next to Plummer's. Greaseball was given an opportunity to account for himself. Seeing what that had gained Weasel-Snout, he instead denied everything. Jane testified that he had been one of the men who robbed her and Lo on the trail. Not surprisingly, Jane's detailed testimony was given more weight than Greaseball's categorical denial, and he was convicted. It was argued whether he should be hung or only banished as he was not known to have participated in any murder, only robbery. The matter hung in the balance for some time until Smith took up his cause and argued for banishment. The men were tired of Smith's nonsense, though, and soon Greaseball also swung slowly from the rafters. The crowd's mood was now at a boiling point. Glass-Eye's fate was argued, and the crowd now bellowed to hang him too. Glick argued that he was mentally incompetent, and Sanders expounded forcefully that he had been promised leniency for his testimony, and had been an accessory to crime rather than a perpetrator, so he was banished. Friends provided him with a mule and supplies, and he left town alone in the piercing cold, never to be seen again.

The work of the trial thus ended. The job of ferreting out the remaining criminals who had been named by their cohorts was immediately taken up by the Masons. They pursued these men, facing great privations in the bitter cold. None of the men on Lefty's list were given the benefit of a trial when caught, but all were given a chance to tell their own tale to a tribunal of their captors. Within a few weeks, all had been executed.

Epilogue

"You ready?" Jane asked Lana.

"I'm gonna learn to waltz tonight," said Lana.

"You better stick to your own friends and leave us alone."

"Jane has a boyfriend, Jane has a boyfriend."

"Shut up, Lana," said Jane.

"You look weird in girl's clothes," said Lana.

There was a knock at the door.

"Be back late," Jane told her parents.

"Have fun," said Ma. "We might be there later. Might. Might not."

Jane opened the door, revealing Andrew, face scrubbed nearly to the point that it glowed.

"You look nice in a dress," said Andrew.

Jane gave Lana a look that said, "So there." The trio headed towards town in the fading twilight. Some weeks now after Plummer had been executed, the days were getting longer, though that was the only hint of the coming spring. They crossed the creek and plodded uphill, past the saloons, the stores, the blacksmith shop. Not a gunshot was heard.

Lively violin music flowed from the newly-finished hotel as they approached. Andrew pushed the door open for the girls. The place was packed, save for a dance floor cleared at the center, where couples twirled in unison. All was carefree gaiety, with no visible sign of the grim task that had been completed here so recently. Anyone who had known where to look, though, would have found the tell-tale grooves of the hangman's noose in the cross beams of the ceiling.

The music stopped. Dez, James, and Robert were clustered together in a corner away from the adults, and Dez waved Jane and Andrew over. Lana ran to a little group of girls her age, the ones who collected flowers and greens in the summer. All the town's most prominent citizens were in attendance—Fairweather and Edgar, Mr. and Mrs. Fergus, Ben Ezekial, Mr. Sanders. Robert broke away from his friends for a moment and approached Fairweather. "Thanks again for that," said Robert.

"Wouldn't do at all, you being stiffed for all your hard work," said Fairweather.

"Still, much obliged," said Robert. "You got the other thing?"

"Sure do," said Fairweather. Robert smiled as he took a small bundle from the freshly scrubbed miner.

Doctor Glick arrived and tipped his hat to Jane from across the room. The fiddlers struck up a tune, and Andrew, with mock seriousness, bowed and asked Jane to dance. She, with an awkward curtsy, accepted. Dr. Glick, seeing his opportunity with the teen clique broken, asked Dez to dance, which she graciously accepted. So both couples—two good friends, and a doctor and his nurse—twirled and spun to the music, having a royal good time. Fairweather and Edgar bowed to Lana and one of her little friends. The girls giggled and let the men lead them to the dance floor. Women would always be in short supply in Alder.

When the music stopped, Andrew gave another little bow to Jane. Robert stepped forward. "Um, got something for ya," he said to Jane, holding out the package. Jane was too surprised to move at first.

"Take it, you silly," said Dez.

Jane took the package.

"Come on," said Andrew, "Open it."

Jane slipped off the twine that held the neatly wrapped bundle, and pulled out a brilliant red bandana.

Afterword

This historical fiction is based on two separate histories, melded together out of sequence.

Henry Plummer was both Sheriff and leader of the outlaws in this region, simultaneously. The beginning of his end came when a young man who was delivering a mule named Black Bess was killed by those outlaws in the fashion described in this story, and the body was also found as described. That was the tipping point for the good citizens of the Alder region. They organized around the Masons, who had themselves organized at an earlier funeral, at which was read the passage contained herein. A trial with a thousand men in attendance brought the main characters in that murder to justice. Simple-minded John Franck was tripped up in questioning about the mule, and earned his freedom with his testimony against the others.

The day after the trial, twenty or so vigilantes signed an oath and went after the rest of the gang, including Plummer, who was hung on January 10, 1864. The vigilantes involved felt so strongly about their moral footing that several of them wrote accounts of their actions later, which provided a wealth of background and anecdotes for this tale.

This book is an alternate history in that Martha Canary, later known as Calamity Jane, arrived in the area some months after Plummer's gang had been eradicated. Her family arrived in the Alder area impoverished, apparently too late to participate in the wealth that the early arrivals at Alder attained. In December of 1864, at the age of twelve or so, Martha Canary went begging in the streets, carrying her baby brother and accompanied by her little sister Lana. The Fergus family took them in, fed and clothed them, and had printed in the Montana Post an account which castigated the children's parents for neglecting them so. Charlotte Canary was a wild woman when she lived in Missouri who, faced with poverty in the goldfields, apparently turned to prostitution. Bob Canary was a farmer in Missouri who turned to gambling upon arrival in the Alder area, and was said to be an incompetent one at that. Jane learned later how to deal Faro from Madame Dumont, a colorful character, who ran a house of gambling and prostitution. Andrew Fergus, whom she must have met that night in December, became a prominent cattle rancher later in life.

Calamity Jane was known as a wild woman in her adult years. Her reputation also rests on an instance in which she helped a doctor attend to victims of a smallpox epidemic, with no regard to her own health. It is not a great stretch to think that she learned that sort of selfless service to the community from the Fergus family.

This writer has always wanted details when reading historical fiction, so for those similarly curious, please go to www.bryanney.com.

About the Author

Bryan Ney, M.D., lives in Malibu, California, where he and his wife raised three teenagers. Dr. Ney has nurtured his creative side over the years with his hobbies of photography and writing. He has had a harmless obsession with early Montana history since finding a dusty copy of Nathaniel Langford's *Vigilante Days and Ways* in a Hollywood bookstore in the 1990s. This, his debut novel, evolved from that passion.

To read more about the history and anecdotes that are the basis for a number of the characters and situations contained in this novel, please visit http://www.bryanney.com/.

Made in the USA
Columbia, SC
22 March 2020